MINOR ANGELS

Antoine Volodine

Translated and
with a preface
by Jordan Stump

University of Nebraska Press Lincoln and London

Cet ouvrage, publié dans le cadre d'un programme d'aide à la publication, bénéficie du soutien du Ministère des Affaires étrangères et du Service Culturel de l'Ambassade de France aux Etats-Unis.
This work, published as part of a program of aid for publication, received support from the French Ministry of Foreign Affairs and the Cultural Services of the French Embassy in the United States.

Publication of this book was also assisted by a grant from the National Endowment for the Arts. 🌾

Des anges mineurs © Editions du Seuil, 1999
Translation and preface © 2004 by the Board of Regents of the University of Nebraska
All rights reserved
Manufactured in the United States of America ⊗
set in Quadraat, FontFont
designed by Dika Eckersley
typeset by Bob Reitz
Library of Congress Cataloging-in-Publication Data
Volodine, Antoine.
[Des anges mineurs. English]
Minor angels / Antoine Volodine; translated and with a preface by Jordan Stump.   p.   cm.
ISBN 0-8032-4672-2 (cloth: alk. paper)
I. Stump, Jordan, 1959–
II. Title.
PQ2682.O436D4713 2004
843'.914—dc22
2004007042

Translator's Preface

The garden of French literature is a lush and slightly wild place nowadays, and a profusion of wondrous surprises awaits anyone with a little time to wander through it. There are sunny patches and gloomy hollows, some dazzling perspectives and more than a few labyrinths, but you are unlikely to find your way into any spot quite like the strange, fertile expanse marked out by the novels of Antoine Volodine, nor any corner quite so richly and desolately beautiful, so foreign and yet so disturbingly familiar, as the sprawling little world of *Minor Angels*.

In one sense, *Minor Angels* is a very simple book: it tells the story of a dying planet, and of the desperate efforts of a few last members of a dwindling human race to keep it alive and worth living in, through revivification or revolution or simply through acts of memory. But within that broad frame lies a remarkable array of individual stories, at once fragmentary and satisfyingly whole, at once independent of that larger narrative and intimately bound up with it; and within those smaller stories lies a breathtaking procession of images—moving, terrifying, dreamlike—that echo from one tale to another, creating among those seemingly disconnected destinies a dense network of half-glimpsed potential connections. Inside that simple book, in other words, lies a dizzyingly multiple book, where new complexities appear at every step and turn, new dualities, new paradoxes: a book as rich in humor as it is in horror, vivid in the poetry of its images and withdrawn in the manner of its telling, continually changing but forever echoing back on itself, quietly but intensely depicting an action at once inevitable and continually surprising, a work that is at once one text and forty-nine texts, separate but unpredictably interconnected.

Thus—to restate that latter point more simply—*Minor Angels* is not a novel. Rather, it is an interlocking bundle, singular and plural, of what Volodine calls *narrats* (an invented word that, with the author's kind assistance, I translate here as 'narracts'). Volodine explains the sense of this term in a little preamble to the original French edition:

A narract is what I call a text that is 100 percent postexotic; a narract is what I call a novelistic snapshot that captures a situation, a set of emotions, a conflict forever oscillating between memory and reality, between recollection and imagination. It is a poetic sequence from which all manner of dreams become possible, both for the actors involved and for the reader. In this book you will find forty-nine such prose moments. In each, as on a discreetly doctored photograph, you will glimpse the trace left by an angel. The angels here are insignificant and of no help to the characters. What I call narracts here are forty-nine organized images in which my favorite beggars and animals, along with a number of immortal old women, pause for a moment in their wanderings; for these are also minuscule places of exile, where those I remember and those I love go on existing as best they can. A narract is what I call a short musical piece whose principal reason for being is its music, but also where those I love can rest for a moment before setting off once again on their journey toward nothingness.

Those looking for a definition of the narract as a genre will find few firm specifics in this little paragraph; indeed, it would seem that the narract form is defined not by some set of objective rules that it must obey (in the manner of a sonnet, say) but rather by its ambiguous juxtaposition of the real and the imaginary, by the place it offers to a host of wandering and dispossessed characters, and by the dreams it can elicit in those who come into contact with it. Now, this is not to say that there are no formal parameters to the narracts collected here, but rather that the form of the narract is meant both to depict and to create an experience (exile, uncertainty, dreams) that lies outside conventional boundaries. In other words, if the narract is indeed a fixed form, it is one that serves above all to express a certain (or rather a multiple) unfixed indefinition. And if we now consider *Minor Angels* not as a series of narracts but as one cohesive text, we will find that same troubling coexistence of the fixed and the unfixed, the defined and the undefined, on a much broader scale. For there is a certain objective formal structure to this work—it is divided symmetrically down the middle, with part 49 corresponding in some sense to part 1, part 48 to part 2, and so on—but that cleanly definable system is both underscored and blurred by another, more amorphous system of recurring phrases or numbers or images, repetitions sometimes literal, sometimes transposed or distorted, from which emerges a panoply of stories at once perfectly distinct and inextricably intertwined, literally or otherwise, with those around them, just as each separate character, carefully named and identified, might at any moment meld into another, and just as the depiction of events might at any time slip into a depiction of the narration of those events, and indeed just as the source of those narrations shifts from an external narrator to the central character to, in the last few narracts, a character we have often heard of but whom we never actually see (or so at least the text half-suggests, almost invisibly, through a series of indications as precise as they are uncertain).

All of this makes of *Minor Angels* a work of considerable technical brilliance, a tour de force of the narrative art; but this formal complexity is in no way purely ludic, and in no way gratuitous: it is a necessary expression of the work's insistence on the importance of memory and the interconnectedness of separate existences, as well as a continual reminder of the inevitabilities it seeks to recount. It is also a spur to the creative imagination of the reader, allowing an act of productive discovery that is both a necessary part of the reading of this work and an activity that takes place or that leads somewhere outside the work, somewhere in the domain of invention and dreams. Nor—and this is perhaps the most important point—should this formal complexity be seen as a sign of a difficult book. Nothing could be further from the truth; *Minor Angels* is not simple, and its wonders will be most apparent to those willing to read with some attention and some imagination, but it is in every way a blissfully accessible book, always surprising, exhilarating, and breathtakingly beautiful. It is a very strange book as well: strange in the stories it tells, in the very visual (and oddly familiar) world it shows us, in the distinctive, not-quite-natural tone of its narration, in its mingled imagery of nomadic shaman-ism, egalitarian struggle, postapocalyptic desperation, totalitarian repression, voyages of discovery, acts of rescue and memory. And although it is a sad book, and often wrenching, it is in no way grim, in no way conducive to despair, in no way humorless or perversely fascinated by dejection or hopelessness or abandonment. At times, it is almost hopeful; or at least, it has a kind of faith in the possible (but by no means certain, and by no means necessarily effective) force of simple compassion.

This extraordinary blend of formal intricacy, dreamlike inten-sity, political awareness, and profound fellow-feeling for this world's underlings has characterized Volodine's writing from its beginnings. Born in 1950—halfway through a century of fear, disillusionment, and failed revolutions—he was eighteen years old at the time of the great utopian uprising that rocked France in May 1968, and was understandably marked by that moment and by the possibility of change that it represented; he was no less affected by the later abandonment of those revolutionary ideals among so many of its participants, a disappointment that (however skeptical we must be of the significance of an author's biography) clearly echoes throughout his work. In 1973 he took a post in a public school as a teacher of Russian, a position he occupied for the next fourteen years, vainly struggling for more than a decade to find his way into print. His first novel, *Biographie comparée de Jorian Murgrave*, was finally accepted in 1985 as part of a science-fiction series put out by the fine 'literary' publishers Denoël. Several more texts appeared in this same collection; indeed, his *Rituel du mépris* was awarded the Grand Prix de la Science-Fiction Française in 1987—this despite the fact that Volodine never quite fit into the mold of a science-fiction writer and was soon to stray dramatically from the strictures of that genre, although never abandoning them entirely. Thus, in 1990, his novels began to appear under the banner of the Éditions de Minuit, home to many of the most adventurous writers France has produced in the past sixty years (Samuel Beckett, Nathalie Sarraute, Éric Chevillard, Marie Ndiaye); in those works of the early nineties (*Lisbonne, dernière marge, Alto solo, Le nom des singes*—the latter translated into English by Linda Coverdale under the title *Naming the Jungle*), Volodine constructs a singularly distinctive, coherent, and curious imaginary world, always recognizable and yet always surprising, whose fascinating complexities have only grown in such recent works as *Nuit blanche en Balkhyrie, Vue sur l'ossuaire,* and—most notably, for our purposes—*Des anges mineurs*, first published in the Éditions du Seuil's *Fiction & Cie* series in the fall of 1999.

There is in these later works a preoccupation with everything that falls outside the realms of classification, categorization, and order. Sometimes this might manifest itself as a blurring of the characters' identity; at other times as an erasure of the distinction between the real and the fictional (between, for example, the physical and the fictional authors of his texts), or between different layers of the narration; most insistently, it takes the form of an involvement with the unrecognized, the forgotten, with all those who, in one way or another, find themselves abandoned—if not entirely alone—in an economically, personally, politically, or even geographically marginal place. These are the hallmarks of a vision or an approach or an ethos that Volodine calls 'postexotic.' Like the word 'narract' itself, the rubric 'postexoticism' has all the appearance of a definable term, but in fact its clearest concrete definition is a preoccupation with the undefined, the unseen, the uncertain. Thus, Volodine warns in an interview with the French literary review Prétexte, 'postexoticism does not claim to constitute a literary movement or style.' Rather, it is a sort of insistence, more or less unique to Volodine, on everything that is outside, an exteriority that is the mode of being both of his characters (beggars, failed writers, exiles, utopians) and of his writing, which, as he says, lies 'more or less "outside" the traditional literary filiations, off to one side, although this does not imply a conflictive relationship with existing literature . . . I affirm my right to difference, the right to explore a little land of exile as I like, far from any school, far from any commercial academicism, far from everything. Let us call postexotic the literary production that grows from that place by the side of the road.' Postexoticism thus speaks of the outside, of the excluded and the omitted; but it also speaks resolutely *from* the outside, outside conventions and even definitions. For a particularly elegant formulation of this idea, consider the title of one of Volodine's most recent texts, which we might translate as *Postexoticism in Ten Lessons: Lesson Eleven*. The only lesson that can be given on postexoticism, that title tells us, is the one you will not find in the book of lessons.

Such is the complicated nature of the text you now hold in your hands; but, let me repeat, there is no need to know any of this in order to understand *Minor Angels*. You will find a truly breathtaking intelligence and imagination at work in these pages, but its appreciation requires no struggle and no study; to be understood, this book need only be read.

I will leave it to the reader to imagine the joys and tribulations that accompany the translation of a text as beautifully strange as *Minor Angels*; I will say only that I found it a moving and exhilarating experience. As always, I did not undertake that task alone, and I hereby offer my sincere thanks to all those who made my work possible: Brian Horowitz, Brian Evenson, and particularly Linda

Coverdale, for their unstinting aid and advice; Eleanor Hardin, for her careful and sensitive reading and unerring feel for language; and Antoine Volodine, for his congenial welcome, for his patient and thoughtful replies to a long list of questions, and for giving me the great pleasure of reading and translating this book.

Jordan Stump

1

Enzo Mardirossian

I've got to face it. I don't react the way I used to. I don't weep properly anymore. Something has changed inside me, as it has around me. The streets are deserted. There's scarcely anyone left in the cities, or the countryside, or the forests. The sky is clearer now, but still without color. Years of endless wind have swept away the stench of the mass graves. Some sights still upset me, others don't. Some deaths, others not. I seem to be on the verge of a sob, but nothing comes.

I'll have to go and see the tear-fixer.

My sad evenings I spend secluded before a fragment of window. It's not much of a mirror. I see a dark reflection, further blurred by a lingering trace of brine. I wipe the glass, then my eyes. I see my head, a shape vaguely like a ball, a mask like brittle paper after many years of survival, a tuft of hair also surviving, you have to wonder why. I can hardly bear to look at my face these days, so I turn my eyes toward the room, the things in the room, scattered here and there in the darkness: the furniture, the armchair where I spent the afternoon waiting, thinking of you, the suitcase I use as a dresser, the bags hanging on the wall, the candles. Sometimes, in summer, the darkness outside turns transparent. Then you can make out the fields of debris where people once tried to raise crops. The rye has withered. The apple trees blossom every three years. Their apples are gray.

Day after day I put off my visit to the fixer. His name is Enzo

Mardirossian. He lives sixty kilometers from here, in an area where chemical factories once stood. I know he's alone and heartbroken. People say he's unstable. It's true, a heartbroken man is often a dangerous one.

Nevertheless, I really must make plans for my trip. I'll have to fill my bag with food and antichlorine amulets, and something to help me weep in front of Enzo Mardirossian, however mad he may be. Something to help me weep madly alongside him, shoulder to shoulder. I'll bring along a picture of Bella Mardirossian, and for the tear-fixer and for myself I'll summon up Bella's memory, which is never far from my mind, and I'll offer him the sort of treasures we have around here: a piece of glass, gray apples.

2

Fred Zenfl

Fred Zenfl should have enjoyed a certain prestige among his companions, first as a survivor of the camps, and also as a writer of prose. But for one thing he had no companions left, and for another his books could scarcely be called books, apart from *Die sieben letzte Lieder*, of which several copies were made, and even graced with a cover and a title, giving them a unique place in his oeuvre. Truth to tell, those seven last lieder are also his very worst texts.

Fred Zenfl's stories dealt primarily with the extinction of his species, and also with his own extinction as an individual. A subject apt to arouse the most widespread interest, then; but Fred Zenfl never managed to find a literary form able to place him in full contact with his potential readers, and so, discouraged, he let his projects languish, never to be finished.

One of Fred Zenfl's endless stories began like this:

I will not bow down before death. When it comes, I will be silent, but I will steadfastly deny the possibility of the approaching beggar. It will be a threat without consequence. I will not believe in its reality. I will keep my eyes wide open, as I have so often done in the course of my life, as for instance when I imagine I am not dreaming, and not imprisoned in a nightmare. My eyelids will not be closed without my consent. The images will not be interrupted without my consent. I will keep my consciousness fixed on that point, that negation. I will not waste my strength babbling old nonsense about the beyond or rebirth. I will stick obstinately to my creed, which is to say that I will proclaim extinction to be a phenomenon that no trustworthy witness has ever described from within, and which, consequently, all signs show to be an unobservable and entirely fictive thing. With all my strength I will reject as groundless the hypothesis of death.

I will stand on the railway of my death, jaws and shoulders clenched, hearing the express train bearing down on me, hearing the shriek of the rails, denying and denying the locomotive's impossible approach. I shall not conceal the fact that in my fist I will be clutching a piece of paper on which, in case things turn out badly, I will have carefully written these words: *No matter what happens, let no one be blamed for my life.*

3

Sophie Gironde

Again last night, like twenty-two years ago, I dreamt of Sophie Gironde. She'd drawn me into an adventure that was entirely incompatible with my character and my skills. We were birthing polar bears in the steerage of a steamship. It was early morning. The ship was stalled on calm seas, or maybe still docked, in any case not moving. The sunlight filtered in faintly. The lamps weren't working, nor was the ventilation. A smell of blood drifted in great billows through the gangway, superimposed on the animal odor of the bears. We'd covered the floor with a tarpaulin, now slashed and torn by their claws. There was scarcely room to move. We heard the dull thud of paws slamming against the metal walls, the claws screeching, the polar bears gasping and snorting. They struggled and writhed, growling in a way that struck me as aggressive but didn't seem to trouble Sophie Gironde, who was more used to this sort of situation and perhaps less awed by the ritual or the notion of a coming into the world. No sailor had appeared to lend us a hand, no one had happened along to calm or distract the animals or even simply to take in the spectacle. We would have been grateful for another human presence, something to keep us from feeling we'd been locked in the back rooms of a zoo, walled off from the world outside.

There were three bears. The first had crawled over to one side and sunk to the floor by the entrance to cabin 886. Pressing her flank to the door, she licked her one cub with an affectionate solicitude we found soothing. The other two were enormous, weighed a ton, delivered cub after cub. Sophie Gironde thrust her hands between the haunches, among the sticky paws, and pulled. I looked after the cubs, graceless little creatures, rumpled, dripping foul liquids, virtually blind and motionless. I set them down on the tarpaulin and pinched their umbilical cords, trying my best to do a proper job. Next, wasting no time, I had to raise the newborn to the maternal snout, hold it out toward the maternal tongue and drooling mouth, taking pains not to let it be crushed or bitten. This was something of a struggle for me. Obstetrics has never been my strong suit. The bears grunted and roared and rolled violently this way and that. They slapped at the air, their massive paws slammed into the metal walls, scratched the paint, slammed again. We slipped and staggered over the waxed canvas, made treacherous by the bears' flailings. From time to time Sophie Gironde was knocked over by the bear she was tending, and I hurried to pull her out from under the smothering avalanche of meat and yellow fur. She rose to her feet without a word and went back to her work. Bear cubs littered the floor amid the pools of placenta and puddles of saliva and blood.

We were dirty. We were blinded by our own sweat. We desperately needed fresh air. The sense of enclosure and the suffocating smell of the animals weighed on everyone's nerves. The first bear had stopped sniffing and cleaning her cub. Abandoning it in a corner between two folds of the tarpaulin, she urinated, then suddenly rose to her full height. Growling, she stumbled down the gangway, from one closed fire door to the other. Now and then she fell back on all fours, rubbing her head against a laboring bear or using the tip of her tongue to inspect one of the newborns. Her presence filled the cramped space of the passageway, coming and going, back and forth, forever in the way.

Eventually I realized something wasn't right, just as I did before, twenty-two years ago, just as I often did when Sophie Gironde invited me to share in a moment of complicity. There was something that made the reality of this moment suspect. It was the number of bear cubs we were extracting from their mothers' bellies. A polar bear's litter most commonly numbers one or two, certainly never more than three. And already we had ten or eleven newborns around us, maybe even thirteen or fourteen—it was hard to make an exact count in the dimness and filth—and Sophie Gironde was now once again at work on the third bear. I told her of my doubts. I don't know why, but my speech was full of words and expressions foreign to me, I said 'oilcloth' instead of 'tarpaulin,' I held forth on wombs in a flat, drawling voice. She shot me a sidelong glance but made no reply. It was clear she didn't believe in my existence. I could feel hot foam falling on the nape of my neck. The first bear had come up behind me, and now she loomed over me, roaring.

4

Khrili Gompo

Just before the winter solstice, Khrili Gompo was sent out on his first observation. He'd been training for several decades, and now his time had come. He'd been granted a half-minute's apnea, after which he would have to return. In those thirty seconds he would evaluate the state of the world and gather information on its remaining inhabitants, their culture, and their future. The time they'd allotted him was meager, but as work conditions go, there have been worse.

Arriving on site, Khrili Gompo backed into something solid, which turned out to be a door. Some distance away, a sign informed him that he'd ended up on the Rue des Annelets. The morning was cloudy, but no rain was falling. Khrili Gompo wiped his eyes, still blurred with tears from the journey. That cost him three seconds. He wore the regulation mendicant garb, and, since the street was not a busy one, he reckoned that no passerby would have time to draw near, notice the peculiarity of his face and clothes, and cry out. That's probably the worst part, they'd told him, a crowd gathering around you, shouting, demanding to know your name and intentions.

He huddled on the doorstep of the unknown building, whose walls had a whitish hue. It might have been an elementary school. Beyond the entryway, he could make out an empty space, very likely a hallway. He imagined the rows of coat hooks, a red scarf, and maybe a clock reading fifteen past nine. He heard children's voices. A teacher was leading a group recitation of numbers or syllables. A metal ruler fell to the floor. Several children laughed.

On the opposite sidewalk, a woman was walking a dog, ridiculously pudgy but likeable as it showed signs of an independent spirit. The woman talked to it as they walked.

The dog sniffed noisily at the base of the wall.

'What now? What do you smell?' the woman asked.

The dog made no reply. It resisted her tugs on the leash, sometimes squirming, sometimes attempting to transform itself into an immoveable canine giant. In every possible manner it manifested a desire to go on investigating certain mysteries of the universe with the end of its snout, reserving the right to choose those mysteries for itself. Its mistress was a woman of sexagenarian elegance, shown to full effect by a black sweatsuit concealed beneath a brown woolen overcoat. She pulled sharply on the leash, formed of two interlaced straps, one yellow, one orange. Only with the greatest difficulty could the dog go on sweeping its snout over the sidewalk, but stubbornly it persisted. The woman tugged once again on the two straps. At that moment, her eyes met Gompo's, and then she looked away.

The twenty-seventh second had now come, and Khrili Gompo realized they were already priming the mechanism to reaspirate him. Not as humiliating as the strangulation of a leather collar, to be sure, but far more painful. He grimaced in anticipation. Despite its mistress's exertions, the dog's snout remained pressed to the base of the wall.

'Come on, it's time to go!' the woman suddenly snapped.

She'd glanced at Gompo a second time. Her voice changed.

'All right, come on!' she mumbled. 'Nothing to smell here.'

5

Izmaïl Dawkes

The most recent historical scholarship places the discovery of the Dawkes on a Saturday, Saturday May 25, at around eleven o'clock in the morning.

Commanded by Baltasar Bravo, the expedition had set off the year before, vainly attempting to locate a passage to the Dawkes before the onset of the November storms. When the cold winds began to blow, the explorers retreated to their winter camp, at number 12 on the Rue du Cormatin, where the captain had a cousin with a room to sublet. The crew piled in gamely, facing their bad fortune with good cheer. But in these cramped quarters the men were forced to endure hardships that soon made the atmosphere intolerable. The blizzard howled day and night. Its moan was enough to drive a man mad. The shutters banged; the crewmembers who ventured outside to batten them down were never seen again. Slowly the weeks went by. Several of the men died of scurvy. Others, made vicious by hunger, engaged in mutual slaughter. Dreams of mutiny were fermenting all around him, and if Baltasar Bravo wanted to snuff them out, or drain them of their power, he would have to bring about a magical apparition of fresh meat. The cousin and a cabin boy were cut into slices and eaten. By winter's end only twelve hearties survived out of the thirty-two that had set off at the start. Now they resumed their journey, weakened by their ordeal, thinking of little other than the day they would see their homeland again. Baltasar Bravo had lost the enthusiasm that urged him ever onward in the first few months of the voyage; a cynical melancholy had now descended over him. Thus diminished, they continued on for some time, in no particular direction, changing course with every sudden fit of frustration, every senseless challenge thrown down by a drink-addled crewmember. A number of deaths punctuated the monotony of the voyage. A sailor—of weak constitution, let it be said—was poisoned by a morsel of food he'd found in a vacant lot. Another broke both legs in a fall down a staircase; they had no choice but to shoot him. Baltasar Bravo's aide-de-camp disappeared without a trace. Two days after the first of May, and even though the maps clearly showed them to be on a route that would ultimately lead to the Dawkes, an unfortunate crewman succumbed to despair and hanged himself.

On May 25, about one hour before noon, Izmaïl Dawkes spied eight unidentifiable silhouettes approaching his home. A layer of ragged clothes was the only sign that they still bore some kinship with the human species. It was a Saturday, and Dawkes was using his day off to wash his car. Interrupting his work, he turned off the faucet to watch Baltasar Bravo break away from the others and advance toward him. The discoverer introduced himself. His linguistic skills had deteriorated considerably, and his breath was fetid. Izmaïl Dawkes took a step back, silent, his mouth firmly set, his demeanor composed. He was not by nature a talkative man. Misunderstanding the reasons for this retreat, Baltasar Bravo concluded that he would have to earn Izmaïl Dawkes's trust; he ordered his men to bring out the gifts they'd trundled with them all through their long journey, painstakingly protected against the elements: clean undershirts, a sextant they'd never known how to use, earrings of colored glass, a Mah-Jongg set lacking only six tiles, samples of lipstick, a box of multicolored rubber bands. This they laid on the ground two meters in front of Dawkes, who looked on impassively.

On the other side of the street, Dawkes's brother Faïd had appeared. He was holding a hunting rifle, braced on his hip.

'Need any help, Izmaïl?' he asked.

'No,' said Dawkes.

After a moment, he went into the garage and emerged with a bicycle tire, which he set down before Baltasar Bravo. Some tread was still left on the tire, and in one spot a piece of light-brown inner tube had been tied around it. This was the object the adventurers brought home with them. It can be seen in the Museum of Discoveries, and for many years it constituted the sole proof of a passage to the Dawkes.

Baltasar Bravo and Izmaïl Dawkes stood face to face for five minutes, each having responded to the other's gesture of friendship. Then, having nothing to say to one another, they went their separate ways.

6

Laetitia Scheidmann

History recounts that Laetitia Scheidmann had just celebrated her two-hundredth birthday at Spotted Wheat Nursing Home when she declared her intention to fashion a grandson. This the medical wardens immediately forbade. The old women spent their days staring at the black larches that bordered the grounds, talking to them for hours on end. They counted the crossbills and jackdaws fleeing the uninhabitable regions and heading toward the camps, where life was less grim than elsewhere, and all the while they made plans for the future. By this time they'd realized that they would never die, and they lamented the sad fact that humanity had now entered upon the more-or-less final stage of its fading, when long before, everything had fallen into place for a glorious present, or almost. Under strict surveillance in their experimental home, they lamented the inability of those still surviving to come together in brotherhood and reproduce. They proclaimed that the ideologues in the capital had failed, that they would have to be eliminated wholesale to pave the way for a radical revitalization of the lost egalitarian paradise. It was in this context that the birth of Will Scheidmann was planned. Working as one, the old women would assemble the avenger the world so desperately needed.

Faced with the strident threats of the veterinarians and the director, Laetitia Scheidmann agreed in writing to renounce any hope of a descendant. Perjury before the enemy had never troubled her in the least.

13

She spent the next few months scavenging the dormitories for stray shreds of rag and bits of lint. Then, once the surveillance imposed on her was eased, she sorted her finds, pressed them into a ball, and cross-stitched them together until she had an embryo. Secreting it away inside a pillow, she entrusted it to the Olmès sisters, who set it out in the moonlight to ripen.

In the night, the old women gathered in the dormitories. They pressed close together, striving to form one discrete being, one single grandmother, mumbling magic formulae, their bodies massed to form a sort of anthill that they called the incubator. At the center of this mound, Laetitia Scheidmann and her closest allies fertilized and educated their grandson. Those on the outer fringes took it upon themselves to stand guard in the darkness of the extinguished lights. Several night-nurses ventured into the corridors during this delicate stage of gestation, and, when they returned to make their report, they were already no longer alive.

7

Will Scheidmann

Four or five decades later, Laetitia Scheidmann presided over the tribunal convened for her grandson's trial.

This took place on the high plateaus, one of the rare regions of the globe where exile still had some meaning. The clouds scudded past, eroding the little deserted hills, scuffing the ground as they skimmed by, accompanied day and night by whistling, by a breathy Asiatic flute, by skirling organs. No campground lay within sight, and yet the geography of the place offered an unbroken vista, stretching far into the distance, up to a dark line marking the spot where the steppe began to give way to the taiga. It had been years since any nomad last drove his herd this way.

The tribunal convened outdoors, in a spot some two hundred meters from the yurts, down a trail carved out by the hooves of the livestock. At the center of a small yellowish depression stood a post to which Scheidmann was tied, and against which he would be allowed to lean as the sentence was carried out. The old women sat or squatted on the grass, unhurriedly hearing the case. One session followed upon the last, tediously, since the outcome had been decided long before. The trial had been going on since spring. Scheidmann was bound by a rope that stretched around his stomach and under his shoulders. The rope stank of camel sweat, of fires fueled with dried dung, of fat. The skin diseases that had tormented him since childhood had abruptly redoubled in severity, and from time to time, in the course of the day, his hands were untied so that he could scratch himself. He spoke in his own defense.

'Yes, it was I who signed the decrees that re-established the capitalist system,' he explained, 'and yes, it was I who placed our economy back into the hands of the mafiosi.'

And he spread his arms in an attitude of regret that he hoped would work in his favor when it came time for the verdict. But the old women sat visibly unmoved by his charades, and he let his arms fall to his sides again, then said:

'It's a terrible thing to say, but for years a great many people had been longing for just that.'

And he paused for a few seconds, waiting for the saliva to come back into his mouth after this lie. The fact was that he had consulted no one before taking that step. He alone had argued for the return of the exploitation of man by man, he was the sole perpetrator of the crime. Then he repeated:

'It's a terrible thing to say.'

In the sky the clouds were tearing apart, like livid rags, ripped gowns, trailing scarves, and the mists behind them had gone a more uniform leaden gray. Very occasionally an eagle appeared, not hunting, not circling over a nest of marmots, but speeding straight ahead, migrating toward what was once the region of the camps, very likely lured by the promise of a more abundant supply of food. The days were warmer now, but the old women still sat bundled up in their lambskins, cross-legged, their rifles on their knees, smoking in silence, as if solely preoccupied with the aroma of the herbs and mushrooms packed into their pipes. Baroque embroideries adorned their filthy overcoats, and the palms of their hands, and even their cheeks, for even now they did not entirely neglect their appearance, and some of them, here and there, had made themselves up with chain-stitched needlework.

And so they sat, impassive, facing Will Scheidmann, their tanned skin scarcely more wrinkled than a hundred-year-old's. From time to time Laetitia Scheidmann posed the prisoner a question, or urged him to speak freely, or more clearly, or to be silent for a few hours so that his accusers might reflect on his case.

'Let me remind you,' Scheidmann resumed after such an interruption, and as he spoke he peered into their imperturbable faces, 'let me remind you that in the cities there was nothing left standing but vacant buildings and blackened stumps of what once used to be buildings, and that, in the forests and countryside, we'd long since lost count of the regions where the vegetation had gone mauve, or lilac, or myrtle, and let me also remind you that the livestock had been so to speak carried off on a wind of death and plague, and that you yourselves . . .'

A sudden gust stifled his words. From the grazing lands, the wind brought the braying of camels and an occasional odor of suint. Unanimously the jury narrowed their eyes. Scheidmann tried to read the opacity and gray transparence of their stare, but he found nothing in his grandmothers' eyes. He offered them a gaze that they refused to receive.

'In any case,' he concluded, 'there was nothing left. We had to re-establish something.'

The old women shrugged their shoulders. They sat lost in the hallucinations of their smoking pipes, in memories of union meetings and evenings at the nursing home in the days before capitalism's return, and also in the calculation of the number of bullets they had left for Will Scheidmann's execution, and in the childhood songs now flooding back into their minds, and in their plans for the end of the afternoon: milking the ewes, gathering their dung, setting it out to dry before feeding it to the fire, tidying up the yurts, stirring the curds, lighting the ovens, making the tea.

8

Emilian Bagdachvili

We could scarcely see our hands before our faces, and someone, probably Bagdachvili, asked me to open the window. Making my way toward the tiny rectangle on one wall, I felt for the latch and pushed it aside, first casually, then suddenly leaping back in alarm. There was something strange about the feel of the shutters. My fingers had sunk straight into the wood.

'A trap?' asked Bagdachvili urgently.

'I don't know,' I said.

The shutters were now beginning to droop. The hinges had rusted through, and the wood had decayed. Light came pouring in as the breach slowly widened. The boards fell to the ground with a muffled crash. Outside the cabin there was nothing but dust, and at once a red cloud swelled up before the window. The dust didn't settle, but formed a curtain that billowed and roiled and ponderously writhed, concealing the countryside beyond.

Emilian and Larissa Bagdachvili did not appear to their best advantage in this dim light, stippled with orange and carmine gray. They looked as if they'd been dragged for some distance through bloody clay, left in the sun to dry out and crack up, and only then endowed with some semblance of human form. We were hardly more attractive ourselves. By ourselves I mean Sophie Gironde, which is to say the woman I love, and me. We'd been following alongside the Bagdachvilis, without enthusiasm or pleasure, since the entrance to the tunnel.

No way out had been cut from the pine-log walls. We found ourselves in a space without doors. The only exits were the window and the trap door by which we'd entered. On occasion, the cabin's occupant might have climbed through the window to come in or go out, but in all likelihood he generally used the tunnel.

The cabin's occupant answered to the name of Fred Zenfl. He'd put an end to his life a few months before. We knew little more of him than that. I don't recall Bagdachvili ever bringing us together before this operation; it was in the tunnel, as we felt our way through the darkness, that he first told us of Zenfl. He himself, Bagdachvili, admitted that his knowledge of Zenfl was purely second-hand, distorted and unreliable. Fred Zenfl had lived a discreet and quiet life, mostly in prison, where, teaching himself from sketchy manuals, he'd learned a number of exotic languages. He wrote short texts of palpable gloominess, never having resigned himself to the crumbling of humanism, and had thus authored several collections of stories, unfinished, autobiographical, and rather mediocre. In truth, Zenfl was more a linguist than a creator. He preferred dictionaries to novels. After his liberation, he'd come up with the idea of compiling a lexicon of slang terms from the camps. This was what he was working on just before his suicide. Bagdachvili's sources had gone on to mention another specialty of his: wary of the nature of the reality he was forced to inhabit, he defended the security of his oneiric realms by laying traps for any intruders who might find their way in, metaphysical flypaper, snares for the unwary.

Bagdachvili scanned the cabin's interior. It was almost empty, furnished only with a cot, a chair, and a table. A manila folder and two notebooks lay atop the latter. As Bagdachvili passed by, a series of creaking mechanisms lurched into action, pelting him with giant tarantulas that might have clung to him and made themselves unpleasant had they not long since become mummified in their lairs. Sophie Gironde had never found herself in the presence of a spider without something unfathomable inside her coming to the fore. She observed those black reboundings off Bagdachvili's legs, those black scatterings over the floor, and she bit her lip.

Bagdachvili's sister went and rested her forearm on the windowsill. Little by little, the dust cloud was clearing. Beyond the young woman's very gray hair, the outside lay revealed at last, and now we could take in the panorama that Fred Zenfl surveyed day after day on his return from the camps: rust-colored dunes, an arid field, a railway line, a signal-post atop which someone had rigged a windmill wheel.

'We might as well not have come,' said Bagdachvili.

We were all disappointed. Bagdachvili had sat down at the table, and now he was paging through the notebooks blackened with Zenfl's handwriting, the hand of an ex-prisoner, tired and dejected, still immature despite the experience of several decades' incarceration.

Scorpions rained down over Bagdachvili's bald head from a receptacle concealed in the ceiling. For a moment, no other sound could be heard than the pages rustling under Bagdachvili's hands and the quiet patter of arthropods, like a faucet dripping into a sink. The creatures were inactive, inert, no doubt dead as well. They landed on Bagdachvili or on the table. Bagdachvili sent them flying to join the spiders' shriveled cadavers.

Now and then the scorpions caught in the wool of Bagdachvili's sweater. He swiftly detached them, never taking his eyes off the pages before him as he brushed them away.

He was sitting with his back to us. After a minute, his voice could be heard once more.

'He's only got one slang term for barbed wire,' he murmured.

'And what is it?' asked Larissa.

Her brother made no reply. He began a vague shrug of the shoulders, then suddenly froze, as if paralyzed.

We stood motionless as well, for some time, saying nothing, thinking nothing. The minutes passed.

Some of the cadavers on the floor had begun to stir clumsily.

Their systems might have been reacting to the light, or to the odor of crushed flint, or to the sounds emerging from our mouths.

Those creatures scrabbling over the floorboards meant nothing good to me.

'Sophie,' I said.

I had some difficulty speaking. Nothing came to my lips but a few scattered phrases of Khmer, a language of which I know next to nothing. I would have liked to come closer to Sophie Gironde, to flee, to embrace her.

She'd gone off somewhere. I don't know where.

9

Evon Zwogg

Khrili Gompo stood straight and silent, in the attitude of the observer, beneath the arcades of the Boulevard de l'Hôpital. He'd been told he would end up in front of a bookstore, but it was a shoe store that he found before him. Given that this was no longer his first mission, they'd granted him a three-minute dive. His mendicant-friar rags reeked with the various odors of his voyage, to the evident discomfort of the passers-by. He feigned a close scrutiny of the luxurious footwear displayed in the window, their reinforced uppers, their double soles, their astronomical price tags. The interior of the shop could be seen amid the reflections. Squatting at a customer's feet, the saleswoman threw him an acerbic glance, then turned away. Her legs were pudgy, and the stippling on her stockings first seemed a symptom of some skin disease, and only later a decorative motif. Khrili Gompo absorbed himself in an examination of the tags on the sale items. Nineteen seconds had already passed.

Evon Zwogg approached from the right. He stopped before the shop window, looked at his watch, and settled in to wait. Judging by his demeanor, he might well have worked in a bureau of applied psychology, as a guinea pig rather than an analyst. He'd come here to meet someone, who was now late. He waited a half minute before checking his watch again.

At the fifty-first second an ambulance screamed past, speeding toward the hospital. Evon Zwogg stepped away from the window, strode anxiously to the end of the arcade, and watched the ambulance disappear down the street, as if he had some acquaintance with the medics or the patient.

Khrili Gompo stood quietly, two meters away. He noted the nervous shivers of the man's shoulders, and all at once he saw him leap back, groaning, shielding his upper body beneath the shelter of the arcades, as one might when struck by a bullet or an arrow, suddenly racked by pain and surprise.

No enemy projectile had pierced Evon Zwogg's flesh. Nevertheless, his forehead was now splashed with a greenish substance, leaving a smear from his hairline to his left eyebrow. A portion of this same matter had pursued its vertical trajectory, and then, after a passing spatter on Evon Zwogg's chin, come to rest on the front of his jacket.

Evon Zwogg staggered briefly, raised his hand to his face, protested with some violence, and frantically searched his person for a tissue. His gestures were those of the motor-impaired, for now his fingers were soiled, and he was anxious to avoid touching his clothes. Gingerly exploring a pocket, he muttered imprecations in a tone of unconcealed rage. The city government was social-democrat, and it took its share of his fury, but his most emphatic maledictions were aimed at social democracy in general, along with all architects imbecilic enough to put ledges over arcades.

Disturbingly, Evon Zwogg refused to consider the most obvious hypothesis, which was that a pigeon had defecated on him. He dabbed at himself, groaning in disgust, all the while wondering aloud what sort of beast could have done such a thing. He reeled off the names of various avians, various mammals, even various sitting ministers. Some of them were repugnant. He went to observe the perch from which the dropping had fallen; failing to discover the culprit, he returned to the shelter of the arches and broke into a fresh torrent of lamentations. His expression was wild. Pursuing his ablutions, he thought it increasingly obvious that he'd fallen prey to a conspiracy, and he said so out loud.

Now he shot Khrili Gompo a look in which, behind his grief at the fate he'd been dealt, lay a mute appeal for approval, perhaps for assassinations to come, or perhaps for an ambitious arson campaign against poultry yards and city offices.

'Did you see that?' he said.

It was already the hundred seventy-ninth second. Khrili Gompo had been authorized to exhale once, in the form of a short sentence or interjection.

'Those pigeons! . . .' said Gompo.

The other gave a violent start. He tossed his crumpled tissue into the gutter. His mouth was contorted with hatred.

'Who knows, who knows? Was it a pigeon? Or was it a cow? . . . Or one of those capitalist gangsters who rule over us?'

He drew nearer to Gompo. He shouted:

'Or maybe it was an extraterrestrial?'

Khrili Gompo had played no part in this incident, he had spewed no fecal liquid over anyone at all; nor was he, in the strictest sense, an extraterrestrial, but he blushed, as if stung by a bitter reproach addressed to him alone.

He couldn't stop himself blushing.

Fortunately, the time allotted for his dive was fast running out.

10

Marina Koubalghaï

'Here lies Nikolai Kochkurov, alias Artem Veselyi, here lie the brutes who beat him and the brutes who cracked his skull, here lies the accordion that was playing the 'March of the Komsomols' when the thugs burst in on the festivities, here lies a pool of blood, here lies the glass of tea that no one ever finished, that no one picked up, that sat for so long on the floor by the wall, week after week and month after month, filling with cloudy rainwater, where two wasps drowned on the sixth of May 1938, nearly a year later, here lies Veselyi's novel whose narrator tells of his wish to be sitting near a campfire when the fatal hour comes, near the trees, beside the road, with soldiers singing a Russian song, a melody of haunting beauty, of simple and unparalleled lyricism, here lies the image of the sky on the day of the arrest, almost perfectly pristine, here lies Veselyi's unforgettable novel *Russia Drenched in Blood*, fallen to the floor in the fighting, for Veselyi was no hack, no operetta Communist or timid bureaucrat or under-bureaucrat, and he hadn't yet been broken by the police, the masterpiece fell into the blood as Veselyi struggled, and there it stayed, forgotten, here lie the uniformed goons who knew nothing of Veselyi's writing but typed depositions and other short statements that a bruised and bloodied Veselyi refused to sign, here lies Veselyi's innate heroism, his insatiable need for brotherhood, here lie the epics Veselyi imagined and lived, here lies the stinking chiaroscuro of the cells, the odor of the iron bars, the odor of men pummeled and pounded, here lies the cracking of knuckle against bone, here lie the flights of the crows and the cries of the crows in the pines as the car drew near, here lie the thousands of kilometers traveled toward the sordid East through filth and swamps, here lies Veselyi's trained crow Gorgha, a proud female, magnificently black, who watched as the car approached and drove off again, never leaving her high perch for seven days, and then, accepting that the irreparable had occurred, threw herself to the ground, never once spreading her wings, here lies the insolence of that suicide, here lie the men and women who were Veselyi's friends, the dead now rehabilitated and the dead who never were, here lie his prison brothers, here lie his Party comrades, here lie his comrades in sorrow, here lie the bullets that pierced his adolescent flesh in his combat with the Whites, here lies Veselyi's despair, Veselyi whose Russian pseudonym connotes a gaiety that nothing should ever have marred, here lie the intoxicating pages of epic writing as Artem Veselyi conceived it, here lies the beautiful Marina Koubalghaï, to whom he was not given the chance to say farewell, here lies the day Marina Koubalghaï abandoned all hope that they might see each other once more before they died, here lies the sound of wheels on ice-covered switches, here lies the stranger who touched his shoulder after his death, here lie the heroes who somehow found the strength to fire a bullet into their mouths as the car drew near, here lie the nights of snow and the nights of sun, here lie the nights of man-is-a-wolf-for-man and the nights of vermin, the nights of a cruel little moon, the nights of memories, the nights without light, the nights of impossible silence.'

Each time she said 'Here lies,' Marina Koubalghaï touched her forehead, raising her hand and pointing to the precise area of her skull from which the memory flowed. I didn't entirely trust the specifics of her account, since she'd been reciting this same litany for more than two centuries, always seeking, in her pride and her poetic fervor, to make each new version different from the one before, but I never doubted the quality of the cloth on which she embroidered this reminiscence, I never doubted its veracity. I looked with nostalgia into Marina Koubalghaï's wrinkled face, her withered hands, her bones grown harder than stone, her flesh grown coarse like mine, the gleaming brown skin that covered her, with nostalgia, I say, because I was thinking of the woman she was at twenty, or thirty, in the days of her fabled allure. When I say I, I speak today in the name of Laetitia Scheidmann. I'd finished milking the ewes, and Marina Koubalghaï had come to squat down next to me for a chat, as she often did at this hour. The afternoon was coming to a close, and we had no other chores to do before evening.

Marina Koubalghaï fell silent. She stared at the glow of the setting sun. In the fading light, her eyes had an unearthly clarity.

After a moment she went on, still pointing to something inside her head, 'Here lie the books that Artem Veselyi was never able to finish and those he was never able to write, here lie the confiscated manuscripts, here lies Artem Veselyi's torn shirt and blood-spattered trousers, here lies the violent struggle before which Veselyi never recoiled, here lie Veselyi's passions, here lies the first night with the interrogators, the first night crammed in with the other prisoners, the first night in a tiny cell where all the liquids contained by the human body had flowed, every one without exception, the first night beside a Communist whose teeth had been shattered, each one without exception, here lies the first night of the train journey, and all the nights in a freezing railway wagon, the nights of slumber among corpses, and the first night of contact with madness, and the first night of real solitude, and the night when the promises were finally kept, the first night in the ground.'

11

Djaliya Solaris

Borodine saved the life of a mouse. He'd always liked mice, and it pleased him to think of saving a life. What then transpired showed him that his influence over the destiny of this world's underdogs was minimal, but, for the moment at least, he'd spared the rodent a brief agony that might well have been excruciating. He pulled it from the jaws of an orange cat. He'd cornered the feline in an impasse, between the sink and the trash can. It was just seven o'clock in the morning. The kitchen was still submerged in the serenity of the nocturnal hours, the hours when nothing happens, when everything that lives lies in slumber, when things mold and decay, away from the light, in a silence troubled only by the old refrigerator's motor going on and off with an agonizing clatter. Everything seemed still asleep, apart from Borodine and certain animals. The cat was fat and silken, with plump, white-striped cheeks and an air of utter sovereign disdain for the world. It didn't give up without a struggle. At first it eluded Borodine's clutching hand, but at last, perhaps suddenly visited by a surge of terrified respect, such as humans often inspire in others, it abandoned its resistance. Under its chin came Borodine's begging hand, and the cat casually dropped its gray offering. The mouse was quivering, wet with spittle and fear, and all at once it sank its sharp teeth into one of Borodine's fingers, the last phalange of the right index, the one nearest its jaws. Borodine yelped in protest and clutched the beast all the tighter.

Now Borodine went out, unsure what to do with his captive. A moment later he was in the street, and then he was on the other side.

It was autumn; the linden trees were yellowing, the chestnut trees losing their fruit, and most of the swallows had moved on. The adult males as well. There was far less traffic on the avenues than in summer. As their numbers dwindled, the cars had begun to widen for the winter, and to change their shape; already the steering wheel was neither on the right nor the left, and the driver's seat had migrated with it to the center of the cabin. The cars were generally piloted by women with huge eyes and sparkling golden pupils, their hair gray or translucent, their gaze fixed on the road ahead, never blinking, never smiling, lazily veering onto the sidewalk, as if they found the controls ever so slightly foreign.

One of these women braked to a halt just before Borodine, ending a fifty-meter skid. Her name was Djaliya Solaris, as the plate affixed to the bumper announced.

The asphalt glistened. The car had stopped on the sidewalk, a single pace from Borodine. A discreet clattering of valves could be heard, and the flawless purr of the engine. The headlights were encrusted with insects; the hood bore signs of a recent collision with an owl, suggesting that in other circumstances, in circumstances other than urban, this car could reach a considerable speed. The driver stared with intense impassivity at a point somewhere inside Borodine.

Borodine knew his place in the universe, and found it hard to imagine any contact between himself and the woman at the wheel. He tried to tell himself a story in which she might figure, in which they might both figure, some episode of banal or extraordinary complicity, but nothing took shape in his mind. Women with enormous golden eyes, with long, translucent hair, women who killed owls, were not from the same world as he.

Djaliya Solaris lifted her hand from the wheel in a gesture that, to her mind, could only express an unambiguous invitation, a perfectly legible sign. Borodine walked around the hood of the car. Through the windshield, Djaliya Solaris's eyes continued to stare, emitting amber waves that he didn't know how to interpret. He found himself face to face with that gaze, that vibration, a secret storm whose rhythm and power he could not comprehend, and he lowered his eyes. In her face he found too many unknown sentiments, unverifiable transports of the soul, perhaps a certain openness, an emotional openness, or an imploring appeal, or, on the contrary, rage, or perhaps disgust, or an entomological curiosity, clinical and cold.

Unable to reach any certainty on this point, Borodine thought of placing himself in mental contact with the mouse struggling in his fist and now clawing at the flesh of his fingers. But there too, true communication, communion, even the very concept of communion, withered in the very first second. The animal's snout was clean and uninjured; nevertheless, from the top of its back, where the cat's jaws had clamped down over it, a drop of blood oozed. Finding itself raised toward its captor's mouth and eyes, the mouse wriggled vehemently and fell once again into a feigned coma. 'Poor little idiot,' thought Borodine.

Djaliya Solaris pressed a button. The window nearest Borodine lowered. With a twinge of terror, he looked down the deserted avenue, then leaned into the opening. A scent of precious wood drifted from the car, a perfume of sophora and rosewood.

'Hello, Djaliya. You don't mind if I call you Djaliya?' asked Borodine.

'Give me that,' said Djaliya Solaris.

Her words were ones that anyone could understand, but her intonation was so devoid of decipherable thought that Borodine took fright. Thrusting his hand into the opening, he dropped the little creature on the seat. Djaliya Solaris snatched up the animal exactly one-eleventh of a second after its four tiny paws came to rest on the moleskin; then, not wasting a moment, she sent the window climbing once more toward the roof. She seemed to have no further interest in Borodine. Already the car was moving forward, already it had advanced by a meter, and the front left tire slid elastically off the curb.

Borodine's story ends there. Did Djaliya Solaris strike up a personal relationship with the mouse? Did she eat it? Did she bring about Borodine's disappearance? Did she, after a moment's thought, draw him into the vehicle? And, in this latter case, did she strike up a personal relationship with him? Or did she eat him as well?

12

Varvalia Lodenko

Varvalia Lodenko laid down her rifle, took a deep breath, and said:
'Oh mindless men! Oh spineless women!

'Before us lies the land of the poor, a land whose riches belong
only to the rich, a planet of flayed earth, of forests bled ash-dry,
a planet of filth, a vast expanse of filth, oceans that only the
rich can cross, deserts polluted by the playthings and blunders
of the rich, we see before us cities whose keys lie in the hands
of the multinational mafia, circuses whose clowns are controlled
by the rich, televisions devised for their entertainment and our
stultification, we see before us their great men standing high
atop a pedestal that is nothing other than a barrel of bloody
sweat shed by the poor, or yet to be shed, we see before us the
glorious stars and all-knowing celebrities, who, for all their much-
vaunted dissidence, never once express any opinion that might
in any way undermine the long-term strategies of the rich, we
see before us their democratic values conceived for their own
eternal preservation and our eternal inaction, we see before us the
democratic machinery that obeys their every bidding and deprives
the poor of any meaningful victory, we see before us the targets
they have singled out for our loathing, always subtly, with an
intelligence far beyond our poor-folk understanding and with a gift
for duplicitous language that obliterates our poor-folk wisdom,
we see before us their fight against poverty, their assistance to

the poor, their emergency aid programs, we see before us their free distribution of dollars to keep us poor and them rich, their dismissive economic theories and their ethic of hard labor and their promise of universal riches to come, in twenty generations or twenty thousand years, we see before us their omnipresent organizations and their agents of influence, their spontaneous propagandists, their infinitely expanding media, their heads of family scrupulously faithful to the most luminous principles of social justice as long as their children have a guaranteed place on the right side of the scales, we see before us a cynicism so well oiled that the merest allusion to its existence, not even an attack on its mechanisms, but simply an allusion to its existence, condemns you to a place of invisible marginality, close to madness, far from any drum, far from any follower, I stand before all this, in an empty land, speaking words that expose me to insults and condemnation, we stand before all this, which by rights should stir up a worldwide tempest of rage, a pitiless surge of extremism, ten decades at least of pitiless reorganization and reconstruction by our own rules, free of all religious logic, free of the financial logic of the rich, outside their political philosophies, without a second thought for the howling of their final watchdogs, before all this we have stood for hundreds of years, and still we have not found the way to plant the idea of insurrection, at the same time and on the same date, in the minds of all the billions of poor folk to whom it has never yet occurred, how to make it take root and finally flower. Let us find the way to do this, then, and let us do it.'

Here ended Varvalia Lodenko's speech. Behind the yurt the ewes began to stir. The sound of voices in the darkness had first disturbed them, then lulled them, and now it was the silence that reawakened them.

The old women had lit a fire a few meters from a yurt. The light of the flames reflected off their tanned skin and glowed in the depths of their eyes, staring into the darkness but seeming scarcely open at all. It was a magnificent June night. The constellations could be read from one horizon to the other, and the heat of the day rose up high into the sky, up to the stars, shimmering, bringing with it the odors of the steppe, while flecks of wormwood and nocturnal flies brushed our faces.

Varvalia Lodenko was dressed for travel, in a blue silk jacket and a marmot-fur chasuble, with embroidered trousers donated by Laetitia Scheidmann. From this outfit emerged her very small head, as if shrunk by a team of Jivaros; hoping to lend it a less mummified look, the Olmès sisters had stuffed her cheeks and even her eyelids with rolls of Mongol felt. Her limbs had also been reinforced wherever a crack was found. Her right arm, which in case of a confrontation would have to withstand the weight of the rifle and the force of its recoil, was encased in bracelets ornamented with crow feathers and bear fur by Marina Koubalghaï's hand.

'There,' Varvalia Lodenko sighed. 'That's what I'll say, as an introduction.'

There was a murmur of approval, and then silence fell over them again. The assembly of crones would now meditate for an hour or two, ruminating one last time over Varvalia Lodenko's speech, searching for any awkward spots they might have missed before. Despite all the care they'd collectively lavished on this manifesto, they knew they still had time to correct any lingering flaws before Varvalia set out into the vast world of misery: wordiness, for instance, or slackness of style.

Varvalia Lodenko bent down over the fire. She tossed in a twig.

She was a tiny woman, of wizened appearance; and yet, if everything went according to plan, it was she who would rekindle the spark that would set the plains afire again.

13

Bella Mardirossian

Suddenly the hens on the seventh floor began to cackle, quietly at first, then with hysterical stridence. There was somebody coming, or maybe a fox, or a weasel. Still, the dog hadn't barked.

Bella Mardirossian pushed away the dishrags covering her naked body and sat up on the edge of the bed, bathed in sweat. The light of dawn filtered into the room; the rising sun had just begun to vanquish the darkness. As was often the case in reality or in her dreams, two geckos were watching, motionless, from the ceiling. It was hot, and humid in the way that leaves your hands limp, that starts a trickle of brine under your arms and over your thighs and makes it hard even to breathe. When I say you I am thinking of her, Bella Mardirossian, and no one else, obviously, because no one else lived in the towering building where she made her home.

She hadn't slept well. She remembered opening her eyes several times in the silence and suffocating darkness. This was how her nights went by from May to October, waiting for a coolness and rest that never came. Her windowpanes were long gone, but there was precious little fresh air filtering through the tight weave of the mosquito nets stretched over the holes.

Bella Mardirossian rose and stood for some two seconds, upright and unclothed. She gazed wistfully at the jerry can full of clean water, filled the day before from the tap on the third floor, in the little apartment she used as her bathroom. She would have liked a quick rinse, but there was no time. The hens' raucous cackling urged her to hurry downstairs at once. Grudgingly, she put on the underwear she'd worn the day before and the day before that, and then a sleeveless dress she'd cut from a brown poplin coat. The nonexistence of several buttons left it gaping open at the chest. She kept it closed with a piece of string.

Downstairs, the hens were going wild. The cries and clucking had only grown louder in the last few moments. Bella Mardirossian pulled on her rubber boots and shut the bedroom door behind her. She set off down the hallway, then down the first steps. This was all happening on the eleventh floor, the uppermost one not yet fallen into complete disrepair. It had rained the week before. The steps made a watery sound beneath her feet. She could feel the suction in her legs, as if with every step her booted heels were sinking into bloody mud, then suddenly pulling free. Everywhere, everything was wet. Water streamed over the walls, fed by puddles still stagnating amid the debris on the roof. A broken pipe trickled quietly at the bottom of the elevator shaft. Broad black pools stood on every landing, slowly spreading.

Two flights further down, Bella Mardirossian heard the distant appeals of her dog, from afar, from another building that the dog sometimes visited, reappearing two weeks later starving and exhausted, riddled with vermin, its body covered with bites.

The odor of excrement and poultry was growing. The daylight as well.

After another two flights of stairs, she stood before the hen coops.

The hens were flying this way and that, crashing together, stirring up clouds of stench and pestilence. She could see their frenzied eyes through the bars, their twitching tails, their graceless wings. They showed every sign of an inexplicable terror. The roosts rocked back and forth, encrusted with droppings. Dirty feathers sank or floated to the floor, landing gently amid the guano or suddenly caught up in a fresh whirlwind. Three eggs had been broken, but there was no sign of blood, or of bodies. The hypothesis of invading predators quickly faded from her mind, and a prowler remained only a very remote possibility. For more than a year, no newcomer had appeared in the city.

'What if it's Enzo?' Bella Mardirossian suddenly asked herself. 'Maybe he's managed to reconstitute himself? Maybe he's found a way to come join me?'

'Enzo?' she whispered.

Without much hope, she peered through the broken elevator door, then into the front hall of apartment 702, where a number of coops had been set up, and where someone might have been able to conceal himself if necessary. The hens were no quieter than before. No one answered her calls.

The little window at the end of the hall had been enlarged one day with a pick and mattock, leaving a gaping hole halfway up the wall. Outside, the sun was slowly emerging into the world. Bella Mardirossian went to stand in the light, opening her eyes to revel in the dazzling brightness, then closing them again.

She couldn't stop wondering: 'Maybe it's Enzo's ghost, trying to appear to me?'

She stood before the landscape, not looking at it, before the magnificent sun, before the empty ruins, before the towering facades standing black in the morning silence, before the expanse of debris, like some megalopolis after the end of civilization and even of barbarism, before the memory of Enzo Mardirossian, before that equally dazzling memory. Brick-red spots floated lazily under her eyelids.

As every day, she thought of throwing herself into the abyss. There was really nothing rational holding her back.

'Enzo,' she murmured. 'Enzo Mardirossian. Little brother. I need you so. I miss you. I miss you so.'

14

Lazare Glomostro

On May 10, precisely at midnight—on May 11, then—the expedition set off. The tillerman had been given orders not to hug the wind, and although at this late hour the breeze was blowing only in meager little puffs, we soon found ourselves beyond the narrows, and speeding westward. We'd lashed ourselves together so as not to be separated and irretrievably scattered in the first minutes of the voyage like the unfortunate oarsmen who had set out to inaugurate this route the year before.

Four hearties stood in the bow, hats doffed, wildly waving their arms as we crossed the Place Mayange and turned into the Boulevard des Ovibosses. But their gesticulations brought no response from the balconies, no spirited 'viva!' to see us on our way, and so they fell silent, and we advanced taciturn into the night. Soon we were nearing the Rue des Sept-Laganes, but just as we were passing by the Chinese laundry on the corner, we were deafened by a fearsome clatter, followed by a no less fearsome silence and a sudden sensation of immobility.

The night was inky black. We peered through the embrasures, tugging at the rope that joined us one to the next, hailing each other, deeply apprehensive. Several of the men struck matches for light, but the flames brought no elucidation. It was forty past one in the morning. We had collided with some sort of obstacle, we were showing signs of a disturbing list, we had ceased to move forward, everything was motionless around us. Happily, the ship's doctor soon confirmed that no crewmembers had been injured.

Djenno Epstein, our acting captain, dispatched one of the old hands toward number 3 of the Rue des Sept-Laganes, with orders to assess the damage, discover its cause, and advise us of our best course of action before morning came, and the rest of the day with it.

This crewman was known in the ports as Lazare Glomostro. We sat down in a circle on the sidewalk to await his return. Concern muted our conversation; after a minute, every tongue had ceased bounding about in its stall. We couldn't help but reflect that the expedition had got off to a bad start. Submerged in the night, we struggled to resuscitate the inner serenity that any creature can enjoy when circumstances are favorable.

After a moment, we fixed our attention on the echoes drifting toward us from the darkness beyond, our eyes and ears working as one, each abetting the other. Sometimes we thought we could make out the distant monologues or terrified cries of the seaman sent out to reconnoiter. From the Boulevard des Ovibosses came a whirring sound as a tram turned onto a switch and continued on toward the General Treasury. At the far end of the Place Mayange, a police car started its siren, or it could have been an ambulance. And so the agitation and unhappiness continued on the shores we'd left behind us, and, meditating on these sounds, ordinary but even now out of reach, more than one of us felt a tug at his heartstrings. Despite the darkness concealing our emotions, some could not hold back their sniffles and manly tears.

Thinking himself responsible for our humor, and sensing that the latter was deteriorating, Djenno Epstein set about trying to distract us. He grumbled three or four rather mawkish folkloric laments, and a few of the men droned faintly to back him up; but no sooner had the chorus gained a bit of amplitude than it collapsed and dwindled away, and as he sang the last song, our captain felt so abandoned by everyone and everything that he gave up on the second couplet. His voice faded, and then he was silent.

For several sweeps of the clock face, no one added a single note, nor a word.

It was then that Lazare Glomostro reappeared, looking older, smelling of bus-station urinals, his clothes in tatters. He settled in next to Djenno Epstein and listlessly told us his tale.

We'd struck a box that was drifting down the odd-numbered side of the street; there was someone sleeping inside it, a certain Khrili Gompo. The force of the collision had ejected him from his temporary shelter and thrown him onto the asphalt. He ended up before number 7 of the Rue des Sept-Laganes. He was still there, still struggling for his life, when Lazare Glomostro came to his rescue. They struck up an acquaintance, they went off in search of a clinic, Khrili Gompo was immediately laid on a gurney, they took him to the radiography department to ascertain whether he might survive his injuries. At his insistence, they took some pictures of Lazare Glomostro as well. With this their friendship was born, with this fraternal photo-shoot beneath the ionizing lamps, this nocturnal sharing of the rays inflicted upon them. After some fifteen weeks in intensive care, and although the interns' prognosis remained grim, Khrili Gompo resolved to make his escape from the medical universe. Aided by Lazare Glomostro, still anxiously camped out nearby, he crept away with no exit pass one night. For the next few months they drifted around the neighborhood of Les Halles, where Glomostro had once met a woman, a certain Lea. Eventually they found her, and she agreed to put them up in her barn on the condition that they cut wood for the winter and not count on her to feed them. Khrili Gompo was slowly recovering, but finally, one very windy day, he vanished for good. Winter and spring went by with no further news of him. Lazare Glomostro then decided to return to his shipmates and make his report.

Sitting near the captain, he searched through the torn pouches and sacks he had draped over his neck in the guise of baggage. He showed them some postcards, the key to the cellar where this Lea woman lived, and then all at once he unrolled a crumpled photocopy depicting Gompo and him in skeletal form, shoulder to shoulder on the radiographic tables. On one side we saw

Lazare Glomostro's frame, impeccable and sound; to its left lay an illegible tangle of organs and bones.

Lazare Glomostro pressed a trembling finger to the photo and said, 'This is my body, This is his, We were about the same age, The photo is a little blurry, He moved, He must have been laughing, He liked to joke, He was a delightful companion in disaster, We were bound by a wonderful friendship, He thought he was going to die, But he must have been telling me a funny story, and I imagine he moved.'

15

Babaïa Schtern

The elevator isn't working, so you have to climb the stairs. Someone set fire to the motor thirty years ago, who we don't know, wanderers maybe, or soldiers, maybe unintentionally, or maybe maliciously, or maybe because somebody thought there was a war on, or a time of vengeance at hand, and that this would help win it, or exact it. Eventually the radioactive fumes and the smell of burned oil dispersed, and now the building is safe to inhabit again. I live on the fourteenth floor, where the damage is slightest.

I always stop on the ninth floor for a rest on my way home. I have to go by number 906 before I can start up the next flight of stairs. There I pause and catch my breath. Someone's been living in this apartment for the past five months. They sawed through the door halfway up, the way they used to do in stables, back when there were horses, and there's a woman who leans out of the upper part, resting her massive arms on the door's lower half. Her name is Babaïa Schtern. She sits there night and day in her nightdress, glistening with sweat, wide and potbellied and smooth and fat as hippopotamuses were, back when there was an Africa. That's where you'll always find her, except when her children push her aside to empty her basin, or pull her into the apartment to groom her or force-feed her.

Perfectly silent apart from the vast sighs or rumbles of intestinal fermentation or the soft hiss of urine or diarrhea, she sits motionless atop a mound of old tires. The Schtern sons piled them up to make their mother a comfortable seat over her basin, with a view of the comings and goings. Still, there's really very little to see, since no one lives on the floors above her but me. Like a sentinel left behind in an outpost far from the front, Babaïa Schtern often glimpses nothing on the horizon for hours on end. She watches over the dusty staircase, the steps that no one ever treads but me, because her sons come in and go out on another side of the building. They use a ladder to climb down to the eighth floor. She sits contemplating the absolute absence of any event, inert, her expression morose, never wiping away the trickles of sweat, feeling the fat slowly congealing within her, sensing the muscle masses distending inside her, rarely blinking, sometimes assailed by aggressive insects, sometimes pestered by moths or flies. The void before her is vaguely fetid, and she takes it in with little sniffs, exploring it. There are nests of geckos in the cracked wall before her. She knows them all by heart, she knows the worth of each, which one is clumsy, which good at languages, which will never overcome its childhood traumas. She loves them.

Nothing goes on above her once I've left the building, so Babaïa Schtern turns her attention to the levels below, to the street, where from time to time interesting sounds can be heard drifting past, the sound of footsteps, the voices of nomads dragging their loads through the ashes and sand. She also listens to the wind whistling through the empty rooms, the songs of the wind, the cackling of the hens in a house where they say Bella Mardirossian keeps a flock. The time passes. Often a long half-day goes by this way, or even a full day, before Babaïa Schtern can look on a human face, which is to say mine.

As I pass by number 906, my eyes meet Babaïa Schtern's gaze, the horrified avidity of her gaze seeking out my own. I never lower my eyes. I stand for a few seconds facing her, I take in her silent meditation that existence fundamentally stinks. I say nothing, I have no answer for her questions. For so many years, no one has been able to say why existence must gravitate around such a cruel and stinking core. I nod my head, I smile, my lips quiver. I feel compassion for this woman, but there's nothing I can do for her. She tries to speak, and I put my body into a stance that suggests readiness to listen, but almost immediately she throws a guilty glance behind her, into the apartment where her sons live, and, just as she is about to deliver a message, she gives up. She heaves a phenomenally heavy sigh. Her sudden distress filters through her obesity, and one of the Schtern sons can be heard clearing his throat somewhere in the kitchen. Another clinks a spoon against a bowl. Babaïa Schtern falls back into her gloomy contemplation of the geckos clawing at the broken-down doorway to number 912.

To the Schtern sons I say nothing beyond what simple courtesy demands. I don't know the first thing about them, even though they're my neighbors now. I'm sorry they've come here. They inspire no sympathy in me. We're just not on the same wavelength. It's perfectly obvious that they're fattening up their mother for cannibalistic purposes. In a few weeks they'll bleed her dry and cook her. It's true that existence fundamentally stinks, but all the same, they could find somewhere else to do this.

16

Lydia Mavrani

The girl was coming toward me, straight toward me, never taking her eyes off my face, her gaze both dark and limpid, with
something desperately intense burning inside it, something more
powerful than any cry, she cut through the crowd. Around us milled
a haggard mass, between us stood dozens of men and women
in filthy clothes, in hole-riddled jackets, in tattered remnants of
dresses or overcoats, in the throng there seemed no way to move
forward. It was nearly two o'clock, the sun was beating down, the
smells of the market growing ever riper, rot was overtaking the per-
ishables, dust clung to the living bodies of the shoppers and rained
onto the dead bodies of the animals offered up for sale in the form
of slices or carcasses, skinned or partially skinned, or in the form
of pieces fallen to the ground and trampled underfoot, the color
of ocher soil and hessian, meat can take on such a color, and here
it had. Further on, beneath grimy awnings, a collection of bric-
a-brac was displayed, principally of a utilitarian nature, tools and
utensils, infinitely worn, summarily repaired over many centuries.
The vendors called out the prices in a guttural croak or falsetto, its
terrible stridence meant to attract the customer's attention. This
polyphony was accompanied by handclaps and punctuated with
blows on improvised instruments, lids, cans, containers, and soon
became irritating. The crowd managed to ignore it, obeying other
rules, undulating in its own autonomous way, without rhythm,
almost impenetrable, shot through with currents both principal

and secondary, eddies both minor and major, forcefully thwarting every movement counter to the collective flow. If you wanted to do business with a merchant, you had to struggle against the surge of the passers-by, gripping the display case, or struggling to make your way under it, a challenge in itself, as it was there that most of the indigent second-hand merchants plied their trade. There, in the butchers' section for instance, scraps of fatty meat and tripe scrapings and ham rinds were introduced into the commercial circuit; in the area reserved for recovered hardware, the vendors offered half-nails, crumbling hinges, iron filings or fragments of rust collected in the bottom of a can. The best way was to come through this front line at a squat, and then stand upright again. Once past the display cases, if you weren't immediately chased off by the butcher, you could submit a price to the counter-clerk's baleful disdain, and so launch into a quarrel over the quality of the piece, and its weight. Here, in noisy, knife-filled dankness, the master-slaughterers and tripe butchers reigned. The air stank of blood, of game-hunters, of the filthy rags they used to wrap the venison. I was neither a buyer nor a seller. When I say I, it goes without saying that my thoughts are of Khrili Gompo. They'd given me twelve minutes. The girl came unambiguously toward me, she came toward me as if she knew me, as if she'd long been awaiting me, as if she'd passionately loved and awaited me, as if she'd always loved me, as if, in spite of overwhelming evidence and endless lectures from her loved ones, she'd held on to her belief that I was not dead, or that I would one day escape the grip of death and return, as if I'd finally returned to her, after a long absence, after a long, very long journey. I stood motionless near a vendor's stand, shielded by a concrete pillar from the brutal and unpredictable movements of the crowd. The owner of this humble concern dealt in chicken heads and other treasures such as lighters and batteries, as well as cassette tapes of Varvalia Lodenko reciting her tracts. I still had eight minutes before me. Varvalia Lodenko was screeching incendiary prose from a squalling portable tape-recorder. The girl

46

broke through the crowd, and soon she was against me. She was thin, lively in her movements, a lively skeleton, an active, southern face, piercing eyes, alert, very black, very brilliant. Until that moment she'd shown every sign of a hallucinatory determination, but when she finally reached me I saw her emotion overtake her. Her lips stammered out a terrible silence, her cheeks quivered, tears dampened her gaze. Finally she got hold of herself. She hesitated for a moment, not wanting to speak, not wanting to interrupt a miracle, perhaps doubting the reality of the encounter now taking place. All at once, she seemed to lose her faith in our two existences. The crowd carried her three or four meters away, swept her out of range, but after a moment she fought her way back, and this time she clung to me. Her only clothes were a tattered dress, damaged from its contact with the other rags in the crush, in the filth and dust. Most of its buttons had been ripped away, and the fabric was coming unstitched in a diagonal line. She tore it further and opened it wide, the better to press close against me. I myself was naked from the waist up, in my ragged shirt. She let out a sigh and wrapped her arms around my back. She squeezed me, her hands perfectly still. We embraced without a word. I could feel her burning breast against mine. I opened my shirt, fearing that the coarse fabric might chafe her unprotected nipples. She stood back as I pulled it aside, then nestled against me more intimately still. She breathed like a woman asleep. Our sweat intermingled. Soon, despite the roar of the marketplace and the vendors' relentless, piercing enticements, I could hear the sound, like a boat at anchor, produced by the pressure of our two bodies one against the other, the sound of rough flesh sliding against smooth, a mingling of sweat, that clapping of little waves, the clapping of love made by loving bodies in an embrace. I heard that. Next to us was the man who sold the Varvalia Lodenko cassettes. He pulled at my sleeve, urging me to lend an ear to the insurrectional appeals the tricentenarian was tirelessly bellowing from his defective loudspeakers, and then, indelicately, he suddenly confided that he too enjoyed that particular noise when he caressed his wife, when he lay down atop her, a sound like the quiet murmur of a canoe. My time was running out. Ten minutes had gone by already. I made no reply to the vendor. I made no reply to the vendor and I didn't know how to console this woman, who had mistaken me for someone else. I didn't know how to avoid abusing her trust, her mistake, I didn't know how to care for her. I decided to ask her a question; I still had air in my lungs, and could speak a sentence with no great difficulty. 'Who are you? Tell me,' I whispered into her nape. She didn't jump, but drew back her face and looked into mine, searching my eyes, exploring them uncomprehendingly, and then she said, 'I'm Lydia, Lydia Mavrani. But you . . . but . . . you aren't Yitzhak Mavrani? You don't . . . You don't remember that you're Yitzhak Mavrani? . . .' I said nothing, I couldn't imagine how to soften her pain, how to ease her distress. The girl began to tremble terribly. I still had more than a minute to go, which was a long time.

Behind us Varvalia Lodenko continued to explain to her audience why we must slit the throats of the capitalists and put an end to the circulation of dollars, and then reinstate a society founded solely on brotherhood.

Lydia Mavrani looked at me with wild eyes.

It was an extremely long minute.

17

Yaliane Heifetz

Laetitia Scheidmann poured a double goblet of fermented camel's milk into her grandson's mouth, to give him courage as he faced the hail of bullets. Then she hurried off to her firing post. Other grandmothers, Yaliane Heifetz among them, then came forward with yet more drinks for the condemned man. Will Scheidmann never said no, he accepted each trembling offering: ewe's milk liquor, Yaliane Heifetz's mare's milk liquor, another sort of rotgut made from camel's milk three times distilled. The liquids spilled from their containers or trickled from the corners of his mouth, dampening his chest, his hips, even his legs. A series of sour-tasting belches sent him into a coughing fit; then, after a hiccup, he vomited an excess of yogurt onto his shirt, which was already wet down to his belt. The old women then did as Laetitia Scheidmann had done: they walked off and lay down with their rifles in the grass, some distance away.

Without the aid of these drinks, Scheidmann might perhaps have viewed his future with some pessimism, but the alcohol had had its effect, and rather than struggling and howling in rage or supplication, he examined his surroundings with drunken dullness. His features relaxed, and an expression of careless fatalism came over his face. He looked at the sky, still gray, he breathed in the odors of the fermented milk, superimposed over the smell of his clothes and body, a rich blend of excremental anguish and sweat, and he looked blinkingly around him like a newborn, or, more precisely, as if none of this had any meaning. Owing perhaps to his drunkenness, the endless itching caused by his skin ailments had eased to the point of becoming forgettable, and he had indeed forgotten it. No longer did he struggle to scratch himself, no longer did he writhe within his bonds in hopes of tearing off the parasitical flaps of skin that had sprouted from his shoulder blades during the night. He scarcely moved. He stood slumped against the execution post that had served as his support all through the many interminable months of the trial, now become a natural appendage of his person, a second spinal column, perfectly inflexible, far more reliable than the first. He slouched and belched.

The vault of the heavens was clear and bright, with a scattering of clouds and two or three last stars. The steppe spread out endlessly, still somewhat colorless, monotonous from one end to the other, but transmitting to all present a tremendous epic desire to live, and to go on living forever. An invisible bird chirped somewhere between the grass and the stratus clouds, a sharp wind blew once or twice, then everything fell silent. After a moment the sun appeared, and then it rose.

Now Will Scheidmann stood waiting for his sentence to be carried out. They'd told him it would be at first light rather than dawn.

His position had softened over the passing months, and now he embraced his judges' thinking one hundred percent. Toward the end, he'd given up trying to justify his actions, or to bolster his case with a list of attenuating circumstances. On the contrary, he'd come to concur wholeheartedly with the terms of the accusation. Increasingly, he only took the floor to heap ashes on his own head. He had betrayed his begetters, he admitted it, and he had betrayed society as a whole. Back at Spotted Wheat, the old women had planned out his future as a savior, they'd given him life to accomplish what they no longer could. 'You gave me life,' he sometimes said, 'so that I might reset the timers of disaster to zero, you wanted me to invent new mechanisms, to unstick the paralyzed gears of the system, you cast me into the world so that I might purge the system of the monsters that prospered within it,' but they had not incubated him and stitched him and educated him so that he might foster the enemy's resurrection, and certainly not so that he might restore the mechanisms of capitalism, the obsolete machinery of injustice and unhappiness whose functioning the old women had stilled forever, in their youth, in the past, 'And that is why,' he said, 'I ask that the accused be given the most extreme sanction in the arsenal of capital punishments, Punish me for the felony of which Will Scheidmann has made himself guilty in your eyes,' he insisted, 'erase me from the ranks of the wrongdoers, as if I myself were the boss of the bosses or the commander-in-chief of the entire capitalist Mafia,' but above all they were punishing him for the crime against humanity he had committed by forcing humankind once more down the horrific road of the market society, burdened once more with the yoke of the mafiosi, of the bankers, of the warmongering wolves, 'I realize that I have driven humanity back into barbarity,' he lamented, 'that I reinstated the cruel chaos of capitalism, that I delivered the poor into the hands of the rich and their henchmen, even as humanity stood at the very edge of the precipice, very nearly extinct, having at least rid ourselves once and for all of the rich and their henchmen,' and he continued, 'In those few short years I threw away centuries of liberating sacrifices and desperate struggles and just plain sacrifices.'

Unknown martyrs and anonymous martyred peoples spoke through the voice of the old women, and now they spoke through the voice of Will Scheidmann. In unison they demanded an exemplary punishment. He presented the case for his own guilt, banishing every last trace of compassion.

'Death by pickaxe in a puddle of urine would be too good for me,' he said. 'Swift execution is too easy for the perpetrator of a historical outrage as massive and flagrant as mine. A hail of stones or bullets would be too gentle a sanction against such a crime; you must find something more painful than death, you must devise something worse than eternal torment and remorse, worse than an eternity of aimless wandering. Lock me away in the deepest pit of hell, never let me out, and see that no one ever thinks of pitying me, until the stars have gone cold at last.'

This was what he said again and again in the trial's final stages, whenever he was given the chance to speak. These were the words he declaimed as his epidermis pursued its metamorphosis, as he stood lashed to the post, enveloped in his own odors of suint, urine, and intestinal spatters.

The aged executioners had settled in at their firing posts, some two hundred fifty meters away. They lay stretched out flat on the ground, in the sniper position. From where he stood, Scheidmann could make out their colorless hair and their headbands and red circlets and the feathered and pearled bonnets that some of them wore, but he couldn't distinguish their faces among the tussocks of grass. Beyond them, the sunbeams picked out the marvelous decorative motifs on a few of the yurts. He could also see the camels, the ewes peacefully grazing beyond the line of old women. A sudden glint revealed the presence of the metal plate that Laetitia Scheidmann bound to her forehead for days of shamanism or internationalist festivals, the very one she'd donned at Spotted Wheat the day she embarked on her grandson's gestation. Then he recognized Yaliane Heifetz's carbine and the Olmès sisters' twin rifles.

It was the tenth of July.

A bird was now hovering over the ewes, and from time to time it chirped or whistled a brief note.

Then the first volley resounded, very likely initiated by Yaliane Heifetz.

Lake Hövsgöl lay far away, beyond the horizon and an immense expanse of taiga, but sometimes aquatic birds found their way to this distant spot, and, as they pursued their careless quest, they whistled a brief note like this one, very clear, very beautiful.

18

Ioulghaï Thotaï

Among the creatures witnessing Will Scheidmann's execution we may include the ruminants grazing around the yurts, glancing occasionally, and not without indifference, toward the post where Will Scheidmann had vomited up their milk; but, above all, there was a bird who hailed from the shores of Lake Hövsgöl, a wader of merry temperament, often criticized by his fellows for the individualism of his ways. He was amusing himself that morning by flying in tight little loops over the site of these operations, or hovering in place, sometimes over the heads of the camels, sometimes over the heads of the Olmès sisters. His slightly stubby caudal feathers undermined the elegance of his figure, but no matter. He'd spent the night beside a little pond four kilometers away, and he'd chosen to fly in raptor fashion more to satisfy his curiosity than in hopes of spotting some prey. He was a greenshank sandpiper, who had completed two migrations in the course of his life. Thus, in the fall, he'd diagonally traversed the interminable lands of the Mongols and Chinese in order to spend the winter on shorelines of yellow southern mud, near once-flourishing ports now silted in and abandoned; then, in mid-spring, he'd returned to the landscapes he loved best, where none of his fellows ever built their nests: the lonely lakes and high taiga, so dear to escapees and red-breasted bears, as well as to vagabonds fleeing the ruins of the industrial cities forever. Having met no suitably like-minded companions that summer, he'd decided to do some traveling, to spend the month of July on the high plateaus before migrating once again toward the Mekong or the Pearl River. Among the greenshanks, this wader went by the name Ioulghaï Thotaï.

He heard the crack of Yaliane Heifetz's rifle; a moment later, a splinter of wood went flying, not far from Will Scheidmann's cheek. A moment later the Olmès sisters fired, and then came a great salvo, melding the simultaneous shots of Laetitia Scheidmann, Lilly Young, Solange Bud, Esther Wundersee, Sabiha Pellegrini, Magda Tetschke, and other pluricentenarians whose identity was masked by the grass, although in fact it was quite short. Then came one final blast, one isolated shot, from the rifle of Nayadja Aghatourane. The bullets whizzed past the condemned man, at several decimeters' distance. Now he no longer moved or hiccupped; he only stood watching, fully aware, despite his manifest drunkenness, of all that made this moment unforgettable.

Ioulghaï Thotaï flew off toward the west and began to beat his wings with sinuous slowness, sinking and gliding as if rounding a funnel, descending so slowly that he seemed to hang motionless in midair, a mode of flight profoundly alien to those of his species, which he'd picked up by observing a buzzard and adapting its movements to his own build and bone structure. Holding his position above Lilly Young, he could hear her throwing out rhetorical questions.

Ejecting the burning-hot cartridges from their rifle-breeches, the old women still lay on the ground in the prone sniper position, seeming somewhat dismayed at their failure to hit the target, and reluctant to attempt a second volley. Black-powder smoke curled beneath their nostrils, mingled with the scent of young wormwood and the insistent stench of ewe and camel urine left by the animals that had slept in this spot night after night for many long months.

Lilly Young spoke of Will Scheidmann and of their memories, their old-woman memories now often ripped and riddled with holes, those holes and rips only spreading as time went by. All at once she asserted that Scheidmann alone could gather up and preserve their memories as the latter continued their slow march to oblivion.

'Here we go, Lilly's off again,' said someone.

'Who will tell us who we are when the day comes that we can no longer say, when no one is left who remembers? . . .' Lilly Young was asking. 'Who will speak of the life we lived in the civilization of the just, how we bolstered and defended it until it was nothing but ruins? . . .'

'Yes, there she goes, she's on that again,' observed Esther Wundersee.

'And she won't be stopping anytime soon, if I know Lilly,' added Solange Bud.

'Who will reckon up our existence in our absence? . . .' Lilly Young continued. 'Who other than Will Scheidmann could recount all the stories of our long lives? . . . Who else could summon up our youth, and then our decline, the calamities, our consignment to the nursing home? . . . And then our resistance, our uprising in the nursing home, our calls for insurrection? . . . Who will be able to tell of all that?'

Ioulghaï Thotaï was gliding ever nearer the ground. He heard every word, he smelled the old women's odor, he saw the grasshoppers and ladybugs meandering over their napes and hips. The old women were now deep in conversation. Four or five of them had already put down their rifles and rolled onto their sides, chewing on stalks of wild barley. Nayadja Aghatourane lit a pipe. Still tied to the post, Will Scheidmann stood nodding, as if he were slowly falling asleep.

'Who will tell the survivors what we were doing here, instead of being dead? . . .' Lilly Young demanded to know.

'It's true, once she gets going, she just won't stop,' said Magda Tetschke.

19

Bashkim Kortchmaz

Without transition, Bashkim Kortchmaz emerged from his slumber and opened his eyes. The moon had assumed its place in the heavens, leaving the night around him not entirely black. He sat up in his bed, watching closely for any detail that might somehow prolong the visions taking place in his mind a moment before. He had traveled far into the past, to a time before the re-establishment of capitalism, and had dreamt of the great love of his life, Solange Bud. In his dream he saw Solange Bud as she was two hundred seventy-two years before, young and alluring, and once again he loved her, once again he'd undressed her as he undressed her then, rediscovering the almost painful harmony that had always reigned between them, from the first day of their adventure to the last, rediscovering, too, the vertiginous complicity and thrumming silence in which they always lost themselves as they made love, and, just before he awoke, he'd spurted semen onto his stomach.

He looked at the time. The little clock showed two in the morning. He arose from his horsehair mattress, took two steps, pushed aside the square of dust rag standing in for the windowpane, and leaned against the sill. Two drops of sperm inched glacially down his left thigh for a moment, and then they coagulated. His breath was rasping, a feeling of desiccation tormented him. The stiff dust rag hung disagreeably next to his head. At the slightest touch, it dropped a shower of mineral particles and glittering dust previously trapped in the weave of the fabric. He coughed.

A great quantity of dust had fallen in the street during the evening, before and after dusk. Cats in heat howled in the shadows five floors below, sometimes throwing themselves on each other and fighting furiously until death or copulation ensued. A baking heat still radiated from the concrete walls. The air had scarcely cooled by three degrees since dusk. A vagabond had recently taken up residence in the house across the street, and he could be heard moving about with a sound of clinks and sweeping, putting his new home in order. His house might well have suffered a more disastrous invasion of dust than Kortchmaz's.

No lamp shone in the surroundings, thanks to the rarefaction of the human populace, and also because no one had found a way to restart the electricity after the last outage. The moon hung round over the apartment buildings, illuminating the Avenue du Deuxième-Vroubel and the battered facades and gaping wounds of the Avenue du Premier-Vroubel. Kortchmaz stepped away from the window to wash off his thighs. He dried himself and was ashamed. As far back as he could remember, these nocturnal soilings had always depressed him, even in the time of the camps and prisons, when existence unfolded in a context of abandonment that stripped every corporeal or intellectual value of its meaning. There are some who, in a spirit at once scientific and roguish, find obscure reasons to pardon this loss of semen during periods of unconsciousness; as for Bashkim Kortchmaz, he resented the manner his system had chosen to fill the void of his sexual poverty. The fact that his dream had reunited him with Solange Bud in no way made up for the humiliation of his incontinence.

His memory of the dream was ripping, falling into irreparable tatters. He tried standing motionless, but already the dream was fading, everything but the nostalgia it brought. His mind teemed with images from another dream of Solange Bud, this one without erotic content. The young woman he'd known two hundred-seventy-two years before was walking toward him in the fog, dressed as a Yakut princess, her face shrouded by the shadow of a hood. There was no way to be sure she truly was Solange Bud in the flesh, and not some other woman confused with Solange Bud in Kortchmaz's memory.

Across the street, the unknown vagabond continued to sweep and shovel the sand. In the lightless silence, these sounds seemed somehow abnormal, and impossible to ignore.

'Suppose I give that insomniac a name?' thought Kortchmaz, once again resting his elbows on the gritty flour that dusted his windowsill, and thinking of names he might confer on him. The rag hung against his shoulder, dirtying the back of his neck.

'Say I call him Robby Malioutine?' he thought. 'Suppose I go and pay a call on him right now, and ask him if he's ever heard of Solange Bud?'

He dressed and headed toward the doorway, where he hesitated. A second assembly of cats was howling in the stairway. Then came a long moment of silence.

His hand on the knob, unable to make up his mind to open the door, Kortchmaz turned and looked behind him. He hadn't lowered the dust rag, and the moon silvered the sparsely furnished room and everything modestly filling it, clothes hanging from nails or a clothesline, a few bags, a bed frame topped with two thin mattresses, plastic basins. From the window a blurred and truncated rectangle was cast onto the floor, next to the bed.

'Wait a minute!' thought Kortchmaz. 'What do I know of this Robby Malioutine? What if, instead of offering me a glass of water and sitting down for a talk about Solange Bud, he takes advantage of the darkness to disembowel me and hang me up to cure in his pantry?'

A fog of silica whirled outside the windows, sweeping left to right and right to left, sometimes producing a microscopic gray spark that glinted off the surrounding dust. The effect was not magical. It suggested something unwholesome. Nevertheless, one could take an interest in these movements; in those minuscule flashes of light one could find an excuse to be fascinated by something, and not to feel one's way downstairs into the street or try to strike up a conversation with a stranger.

Kortchmaz went and sat down on the bed again. For the next hour he watched the dancing dust and listened to the sounds of the night. The cats had gone away. Robby Malioutine had stopped sweeping. Now he was quiet. In the Avenue du Deuxième-Vroubel, a madman shouted that someone had bitten him; he tearfully protested for a minute, then faded back into nothingness. In the distance the motor of a nouveau-riche's generator hummed. As painlessly as he could, Kortchmaz tried to remember Solange Bud as she was two hundred seventy-two years before. And then, once the moon had sunk behind the tall buildings on the Rue du Kanal, he fell asleep again.

20

Robby Malioutine

Contrary to what I'd briefly imagined, Robby Malioutine was not a cannibal; nor, I was soon able to assure myself, was he a nouveau-riche, nor an admirer of the nouveaux-riches, or of the capitalist system. In other words, there was no reason to avoid him. For ten days and nights I observed his ways and habits, and then I went to visit him on the third floor of the building across the street. When I use the first person, it should be understood that I'm thinking principally of myself, which is to say Bashkim Kortchmaz.

From the beginning, our relationship was marked by a total absence of aggression, and by the kind of unexpansive camaraderie that develops among vagrants after a cosmic catastrophe or long before the world revolution.

Malioutine had knocked about in numerous strange locales, here and there, all over the globe. He'd returned with a certain experience of the world, but he disguised his knowledge behind a conversational style composed of banalities, prudent evasions, and lapses of memory. He preferred to keep to the background, never imposing on others the lavishness or horror, no doubt brutal, of the memories packed into his skull. Keeping quiet was a lesson he'd learned in his wanderings through those various paradises or hells, remote or exotic, and then learned again once he'd managed to find his way back. He knew that words can be hurtful to the survivors and irritating to those who failed to survive, that an image is a difficult thing to share, that a disquisition on foreign lands will always come across as a rant or a vain display. Nevertheless, it made him somehow unhappy to conceal a knowledge that, in the end, no one forbade him to divulge, and so he began to give lectures, at a rate of two per month.

Malioutine spoke a Mongol dialect from the western shores of Lake Hövsgöl, and he spoke it with the most spectacular deformations. He borrowed his vocabulary from the Russian, Korean, and Kazakh he'd used in the camps, three hundred years before; in the end, these had come to supplant his own mother tongue, which I suppose, in spite of everything, must have been Darhad. It was in this laborious pidgin that he delivered his lectures.

His talks had two titles: *Luang Prabang: Butterflies and Temples* and *A Journey to Canton*. He gave them together, in a single sitting, first one and then the other, all the while making tea for the men and women who'd come to hear him speak. He hoped this enticing program might attract a large crowd, and when I say enticing I mean it sincerely, for no doubt those two cities were once worth a long journey, and deserved to be brought back to life in words today. Nevertheless, nothing came of his efforts. No one had ever shown any intention of attending these events, and, the evening of the lecture, the room was inevitably empty.

I myself went to hear him speak every time, without fail. We found ourselves alone in the room, swept for the occasion with maniacal care. His door stood wide open, and a garland of red ribbons and rags hung over the building's entrance to attract the public's attention and help the audience find its way. Nevertheless, no one ever came trudging up the stairs to his room; no one even came down the street.

The conditions for a real *causerie* not having been met, Malioutine found excuses to stall. I waited in silence, sitting on a clean plank, my gaze fixed on the sheets of photographic paper he'd hung on the wall, their uniform brown tint imparting not the slightest information. At last he made up his mind to begin, and, after clearing his throat, he addressed the audience, which is to say me, and asked if we wanted our tea right away or later on. Then, since I offered no clear response to this question, allowing him to determine the evening's format as he saw fit, he launched into a series of sentences on the subject of Luang Prabang. He informed us that he hadn't succeeded in entering Laos himself, and that his information came to him second-hand, but that, for example, he'd been assured that in certain temples the worshipers used missile shells to hold their bouquets, their offerings of orchids or daisies, of lotus, of ilang-ilang. He never specified the caliber, but he spread out his arms to show the approximate diameter of the copper cylinders. He continued with an enumeration of flowers, not an easy lexicon to master with several idioms competing at once, and then he returned to the central theme of his talk. 'At Luang Prabang,' he said, 'there are pagodas whose vases are missiles.' It took some effort to follow the thread of his speech. He paused, struggling to find a word, sometimes for fifteen or twenty seconds, then tossed out an incomprehensible phrase in Korean slang or Kazakh, and then he fell silent again. The photographs were perfectly monochromatic, their decipherability obliterated by several decades' exposure to the atmospheric or solar rays. Nonetheless, Robby Malioutine made liberal use of them to illustrate his oral depictions, to make his ramblings more real, more pedagogical. He referred to them, he commented on them, albeit turning to face them only for the briefest moment, as if fearing that the audience might take advantage of his momentary inattention to slip out. The exceptionally vague nature of these pictures gave them a universal quality. Through them, one could well imagine oneself in Luang Prabang or in Canton, one or the other, in a pagoda or on a riverbank, on the Mekong, on the Pearl River. The second lecture thus flowed smoothly from the first. Canton should be pronounced Guangzhou, Malioutine was most insistent on that point, and sometimes he demanded active participation from his audience, leading a group repetition of those two Chinese syllables, one on the third tone and the other on the high tone. He had them repeat this name several times. Then it was time for our tea, accompanied by chit-chat of a relatively vacuous nature, and soon we were expressing no further thought worthy of voice.

21

Sorghov Morumnidian

At first it was hard to believe that Sophie Gironde was once more beside me, that I no longer had to wait for some perfect conjunction of dreams to be with her, nor spend three thousand years traversing the slow, dark horrors of hell. I had only to cross a divide of several meters to be near her, I had only to reach out my hand to touch her. That was what surprised me. I reached out my hand for her, I crooked my arm as if in an invitation to dance, and at once I rediscovered the gestures of two lovers meeting, in all their wonderful banality, gestures so often repeated but always offering inexhaustible delights, when neither partner is pretending. No more lifetimes spent languishing; only a moment after I had conceived the desire to do so, I could now caress her shoulder, the small of her back, then finally draw her against me, with a gentleness one can dream of only in dreams, against my mouth and my body, unbelieving after that long void of absence. Sophie Gironde pressed against me, nothing mortally dangerous took form before us, nothing came rushing to wrench us apart, and, as our breath united, I could feel the accessibility of her skin through the cloth, when there was cloth between us, and even, eclipsing our physical harmony, the accessibility of her memory, for we stood quivering on the very edge of words, saying nothing, trembling together, each of us as if on the brink of a mental leap from one to the other. This was what I found hard to believe. I was sure my happiness might still be taken from me without warning, as before, between two blinks of an eyelid. In this case, when I say I, it is above all the identity of Sorghov Morumnidian that I assume. I saw the present as a series of illusions clinging coherently one to the next, including moments of sleep and separation, incorporating all the prosaic events of daily life, and so, in the end, fabricating a perfectly plausible sort of reality, of which we were nevertheless in danger of being stripped by the slightest upheaval of fate. At first, I feared I might lose everything at any moment, and I declared this fear to Sophie Gironde, biting my lips so as not to weep as I spoke. That made her laugh. Then a sort of habituation set in, and, although I couldn't entirely vanquish my skepticism, I pushed it away to one side. My life with Sophie Gironde was a quiet one. We found lodging in long-abandoned hovels, unclaimed houses, we met gallows-birds and people of low condition, fading away around us, like us, and sometimes too we found ourselves in perfect solitude, for a few fleeting moments or, on the contrary, for many years, for many long years. And then our travels began to slow, our journeys grew shorter and essentially circular. We ended up on the banks of an equatorial river, where there seemed no point in continuing the quest for exile. Ripped by the floodwaters from marshy canals or lagoons, huge clumps of water spinach and lilies floated by on the river's brown surface. At daybreak we walked to the marshy riverbank. We circled the puddles, reluctantly abandoned by the snakes as we approached, and we went to reflect before the little lapping waves, enjoying the last hour of relative coolness before the heat returned. The sky was turning a dingy blue. We held hands, watching the ugly tangles float past, the twisted remains of the plant life strewn over the water as far as the eye could see. The banks were low, sometimes impossibly overgrown, sometimes barren and abrupt, depending on the distance we'd walked in the night's final moments. A stench of compost and banana plantations rose from the earth. We stood on the bank watching as the flamingos awoke, as the first boats began crossing the river, back and forth. In the distance, at a bend not yet veiled by haze, we could see a village built on stilts, overlooked by a pagoda of no great resplendence, clearly impoverished, and Sophie Gironde broke the silence to say, 'At Luang Prabang, there are temples whose altar vases are missile shells.' I'd once heard a lecture on this subject, which I knew for a fact Sophie Gironde had not attended, and at such moments I reflected that only my bewitched memory could have put these words between my lover's lips. This was enough to revive my anxieties. Again I sensed an absence of certainties supporting the world around us. The reality of our reunion and the existence of Sophie Gironde had to be viewed with some skepticism. I swallowed, I squeezed Sophie Gironde's hand, my mind full of questions on the present we seemed to be sharing. I consulted my internal calendars, seeking a chronology of the events that had led me to this moment. At the very least, I should have been able to situate this present with respect to a past, to some sort of past, inscribed in my memory. But my calculations led nowhere, no matter how I labored, even when I limited my search to the few preceding days. This I found terrifying, and, in one final act of desperation, I questioned Sophie Gironde. 'Shh,' she answered. 'You're going to frighten our elephants.' 'What elephants?' I asked. I turned around. Behind us I saw the little hill, and our little house atop it, in a clearing that I had no memory of hacking out from the forest, and the herb garden where I couldn't remember growing the mint and coriander that seasoned our meals. The elephants were trampling our plantings, waving their ears. Sophie Gironde took an unmistakable delight in their destructive nonchalance, and, in the glow of the rising sun, she suddenly seemed animated by thoughts and memories both alien and inaccessible. And once again it was all just as it was at the start, hard to believe.

22

Nayadja Aghatourane

The sky burned all day long.

Not a bird could be seen, the blasted prairie was still, even the flies were disappearing. The animals silently looked for shade beside the felt tents. If you were standing in the wrong place, as Will Scheidmann was, the sunlight could blind you the moment you opened your eyes. Camels and ewes drifted over what looked like a lake of molten tin, the yurts undulated behind a shimmering curtain of heat. The old women blended into the landscape, lying motionless amid the gleaming and yellowed or intensely gray seedheads and stalks, hunched over their rifles among molehills, atop rock-hard fragments of dung. Suddenly your retinas felt as though they'd been scorched by flames, and you instinctively closed your eyes. Then you pressed your eyelids together a bit tighter, and little by little your sight returned. In that intimate darkness, it returned.

And now, with night having fallen, you felt more at ease to invent images. Light winds from the steppes swept by here and there. They brought no coolness with them, but at least they didn't blind you.

Will Scheidmann's execution had been underway for three weeks. Ever since that first failed salvo, the condemned man had been waiting for the old women to kill him. But instead of peppering him with bullets, they'd then launched into a debate, trying to decide if they should move nearer the post and start over, or if they'd do better to grant Scheidmann a reprieve, if only to inflict some other punishment, such as forcing him to archive their childhood dreams, now growing sparse through amnesia. There seemed no way to reach a decision. Night and day, still crouched in firing position, they smoked pipes packed with aromatic herbs, all the while exchanging opinions and long silences. Sometimes, especially at night, they arose to defecate in a nearby dale, or went off to milk a ewe suffering from an overabundance of milk, but these absences never lasted long. After a few moments, they could be seen making their way back to the firing line. They offered small bites of cheese to their neighbors, then immediately stretched out on the ground again, as lithe as old wildcats.

Three weeks.

Twenty-one days.

And twenty-one stories, too, that Will Scheidmann conceived and worked in the face of death, for his grandmothers kept their rifles trained on him without letup, whether under the stars or in the blaze of noon, as if to remind him that at any moment the order to open fire might once again spring from the mouth of Laetitia Scheidmann, or Yaliane Heifetz, or another. Twenty-one, and soon twenty-two strange narracts, no more than one each day, composed by Will Scheidmann in your presence, and when I say Will Scheidmann I am of course thinking of myself. And so he now delivered a twenty-second unsummarizable impromptu, with nothing before him but a threatened survivor's delirium and a false tranquility in the face of death, and I fashioned this prose in the same spirit as the ones before, as much for myself as for you, putting you in the spotlight so as to preserve your memory in spite of the wear of the centuries, in hopes that your kingdom will come, for, despite the rather ineffectual nature of my collaboration with you, I felt for your persons and your convictions a tenderness that nothing ever tarnished, and I wished that you might be immortal, or at least more immortal than me.

I fell silent. A grasshopper had leapt onto one of my legs. My trials had brought about a metamorphosis in my body. Flaps of parasitic skin were proliferating all over me, provoked by my nervous diseases. Great ligneous scales and excrescences covered me from head to toe, growing larger every day. The grasshopper had hooked its legs over one of these.

I opened my eyes. The nocturnal steppe lay draped in stars, and then the moon emerged. I would have liked someone to talk to. I would have liked someone to speak to me of the men and women I'd told of, to speak of them with love, with fraternity and compassion, to say to me: 'Yes, I knew Lydia Mavrani, tell me again what she was like after her survival,' or 'Give me news of Bella Mardirossian,' or else 'You really must try to compose an account of Varvalia Lodenko's adventures,' or else 'We also belong to the dying humanity you describe, we too have come to this point, to these final moments of dispersion and nonexistence,' or else 'You were right to show how the joy of remaking the world has been stolen away from us forever.' But there was no one whispering beside me, no one encouraging me to continue. I was alone, and suddenly I began to regret it.

The grasshopper had perched on one of the growths branching out from my right hip. It chirped twice, then leapt onto the rope binding my chest, then chirped again.

The old women still lay before me, perfectly impassive, at an average distance of two hundred thirty-three meters. I would have liked to explain why I was inventing something other than limpid, artless little anecdotes, why I had chosen to bequeath them these narracts with their odd non-conclusions, and by what technique I'd constructed images designed to embed themselves into their unconscious, then emerge again later in their meditations or dreams.

Just then, Nayadja Aghatourane called to me. She was the youngest of the sharpshooters, having celebrated her bicentennial only twenty-seven years before.

'To emerge again later in their dreams,' I was saying.

She sat up, her form unfolding in the moonlight from among the tufts of ginseng and budargana. I saw her wretched marmot-fur coat rising up from the top of a little mound, but with the darkness behind her I couldn't make out the restitchings and the vermillion embellishments and the magic slogans in Uyghur, and I glimpsed her tiny head, as if freeze-dried by age, a little mass of bald, grainy leather whose lower half was reinforced by an iron dental plate, reflecting the stars with every word she spoke.

A special affection bound me to Nayadja Aghatourane. Back when I lay gestating in the nursing home, as I lay concealed, incompletely conceived, beneath the bed of one aged conspirator or another, she was the only grandmother to think of repeating fairy tales into my ears along with the classics of Marxism. I hadn't forgotten that.

'Scheidmann,' she cried, 'what are these strange narracts you're hoodwinking us with? Why strange? . . . Why are they strange?'

I was tired. Weariness prevented me from unsealing my lips, and I made no reply. Despite the horrible torment of my itching flesh, I did not move the ragged mass of skin that enveloped me, which I could feel continually growing under the effect of the lunar gravity. A bolt of heat lightning slashed the sky. For a moment I felt a mad certainty that the old women were about to resume firing and be done with it, and then I realized that, alas, no such thing was true. The waiting started again. I wanted to answer Nayadja Aghatourane, to scream through the hot night that strangeness is the form taken by beauty when beauty has no hope, but I kept my mouth shut, and I waited.

23

Safira Houliaguine

In the nursing home, the nose takes over when the eyesight dims, or when the night is dark. Spotted Wheat's two buildings share the smell of a cuisine based on rotten cabbage and onion, and they also smell of the horsehair cushions on the great room's urine-soaked armchairs, and they also smell of the dental prostheses lying on the nightstands and the brown grime on the brown wainscots, and stale black bread, and the little bitter apples eaten here for dessert, and also the black soap applied to the wood floors downstairs when the warm weather returns, and the dust from the rugs rolled up in the hallway when spring cleaning is underway, and they also smell of the rubber sheets drying in the dormitories every morning, and in the winter they smell of the deep-fried pastries cooked up by fat Ludmilla Matrossian and her daughter Rosa Matrossian every Wednesday of the snowy season, and in the autumn they smell of the pharmaceutical products distilled by the director from certain mushrooms that grow on the tree-stumps, and ever more faintly one can make out the smell of the veterinary apparatuses brought in from the capital, for while experiments were once performed here to study the old women's immortality, the researchers eventually wearied of their long trips to the home, or died, and in any case showed no further interest in the old women except by correspondence, and finally abandoned them, thousands of miles from everything, in the care of specialized nurses, with orders to shoot on sight if they ever attempted to cross the perimeter of their allotted expanse of taiga.

The two buildings house a great many other odors as well, upstairs and down. For instance, you might notice the smell of the illustrated monthly magazines, their covers celebrating the beauty of combine harvesters and crawler tractors, or offering views of the Angara or the Abakan shot from a geologist's raft somewhere in the endless forest, or sometimes groups of young worker-girls, pleasingly plump before a background of fisheries or oil wells or laughing joyously in front of a nuclear plant or a slaughterhouse, charming, bubbling with enthusiasm. And in the air of the two buildings there also hangs the nebulous trace of our hair, and of Ludmilla Matrossian's blue apron, and the smell of cucumber peelings, and a whiff of dishwater, and from the end of the left-hand hallway drifts the persistent odor of the toilets, never really clogged or unclogged, mingling with the smell of the cupboards where abrasives and rat poison are stored, and in the two common rooms you can make out an odor, more tarry than the scent of the four-color magazines, that emanates from the nonillustrated literary revues, where, in sturdy constructions much prized in literature since the end of literature, salaried authors movingly relate the miserable exploits of our generation and of generations before, and of all those who offered up their innate heroism to a society forever striving toward our egalitarian ideal, and of all those who built that ideal brick by brick in spite of the wars and the massacres and the privations and in spite of the camps and the guards in the camps, and went on building it heroically until it wouldn't stand anymore, and even until it would never stand again.

But that's still not all, because there are also the cyclical odors, as for instance the scent of charred dust that suddenly spreads upstairs and down when the central heating is relit in midautumn, or the smell of the birds that fly into the common room in the spring, crashing desperately against the upper corners of the walls, spattering fear and guano over the portraits of the home's founders, nor must we neglect the vegetal odors seeping in from outside, especially the overpowering presence of the resins that ooze from the pines and black larches and bead up on the watchtowers where no soldier stands guard, constructed at our request on the other side of the vegetable garden, to give us a point of reference, so that the imprisonment of our old age wouldn't seem too far removed from the universe of our youth.

There are hundreds of chapters in Spotted Wheat's repertory of scents. To these we might add certain fragrances less universal and more discreet, more intimately linked to one individual destiny or another, such as the odor that greets Yaliane Heifetz's nostrils when she opens the cardboard box where for nearly nineteen decades she has preserved the letters sent by her husband Djorgui Heifetz, four letters mailed on four different dates, but which all reached her together, never to be followed by others. Safira Houliaguine was in charge of the mail in those days. She worked in a back room of the sorting office, watching for correspondence of a delicate nature. She came in person to bring Yaliane Heifetz the four envelopes. It was a Saturday in June. She held them out to Yaliane Heifetz, unable to speak, her hands trembling, and the two women bit their lips until the blood came. The envelopes bore the name of a locality not yet founded in those days, and later wiped from the map: Tungulansk, on the left bank of the Yenissei. From these letters they learned that the first group of huts is going up quickly, that the felling of the trees is proceeding at a good pace, that two bears were recently seen prowling near Lake Hoiba, that the temperature has scarcely once fallen below zero, even though September has already come, and that, to protect them from scurvy, this winter they'll enjoy an abundance of pine nuts and pine cones and even pine needles, which some of the men have already taken to chewing when there's no food to eat. The handwriting is clumsy and broken, as letters in pencil from a camp on the Yenissei always are. Yaliane Heifetz opens the cardboard box and remembers the June afternoon when Safira Houliaguine knocked at her door. She sees her again, white as a sheet, offering her these messages supposedly written by Heifetz's hand. She unfolds the ruined paper, still smelling of the paper of the past, the ink of the past, and also of a certain eau de cologne that Safira Houliaguine favored in those days, with loving care she fingers the sheets, on which no fragrant particle summons up the pines of Lake Hoiba or the real color of the frozen alluvium where great logs were rolled into place to mark out Tungulansk's future site. Neither the envelopes nor the brittle, yellowed paper bear the faintest trace of olfactory information, nor did they ever, which is strange, and which, deep down, places their authenticity in doubt. One hundred ninety years ago, when Yaliane Heifetz first opened them, quivering and breathless, this absence of odor struck her as highly abnormal, even then. Safira Houliaguine stood beside her, equally emotional, her eyes full of tears. 'You didn't write them for him, to console me?' Yaliane Heifetz had asked her friend. In the back room of her mail office, Safira Houliaguine could easily have doctored up a few envelopes, falsified some cancellations, forged Heifetz's tortured handwriting. Safira Houliaguine shook her head, shook her magnificent black braids. And sobs were her only answer.

Yaliane Heifetz rests the cardboard box on her knees and gazes at it for hours, as if forbidding herself to look inside without a long pause beforehand, and then at last she opens it. Scrap by scrap she explores the remnants of paper, the words she knows by heart, now illegible, searching through the last lingering traces of their smell. The paper reveals only what it has always revealed: it had indeed been held and folded or smoothed by human hands, but only her own and Safira Houliaguine's.

Not far away sits Safira Houliaguine, and, as two centuries before, she is trembling from head to toe. 'Do you promise me you didn't write these letters?' Yaliane Heifetz asks once again. 'No, it wasn't me,' Safira Houliaguine insists, for the ten thousandth time. 'You swear?' Yaliane Heifetz goes on. 'Yes, of course, I swear, you know that already,' says Safira Houliaguine, with a tremor in her voice.

24

Sarah Kwong

I've been playing hooky these past few weeks. Rather than head
off every morning for the Koriagin Tower Educational Center, on
the Rue du Kanal, I've been spending my days in the market. I
sit with a Chinese woman as she tries to sell bouquets of herbs
and a few vegetables. When I say a Chinese woman, it should go
without saying that my mind is on Maggy Kwong, with whom I've
been sharing a segment of destiny for a year now. Our mercantile
activities were too paltry to earn the unwavering contempt I'll
always feel for the capitalist system. They demanded no real effort;
I could sit idle for hours once I'd helped Maggy Kwong elegantly
lay out her bundles of medicinal plants, harvested the day before
on the sixth floor or the old railway bridge. Maggy Kwong was like
every Chinese woman I'd ever happened to live with, very pretty,
austerely industrious, unexpansive. We were both close to sixty
years old. From our market stand we viewed the passing tide of
Tungu and German refugees, of Goldes and wretched Russians, of
Buriats and Tuvas, Tibetan refugees and Mongols. Not that there
was ever much of a crowd, just a few scattered sleepwalkers, here
and there. In the slowest hours of the day, there were no shoppers
at all.

I'd decided to give up on school. I was finding I cared less
and less for education. I'd lost the capacity to assimilate new
material, and I wasn't expanding my existing knowledge in any
way. That's how it is: suddenly the taste for learning disinte-

grates, your curiosity goes blunt, you find yourself heading down-hill, and you don't feel sad about it. You sit before an armload of spinach leaves, you keep an eye on the parsley, and you're happy with that. When I say you, you will understand that I am speaking of Yasar Dondog, which is to say me, and no one else.

The Educational Center was directed by Sarah Kwong, Maggy's sister. She and I got along only middlingly. I found it terribly difficult to follow her lessons, and I didn't entirely appreciate her brutal treatment of certain truths I'd always clung to for my survival. Take for instance her course in oral expression. She instructed us to go to the window and observe what was happening in the street, then use what we'd seen to inspire our words. We were rarely more than two or three in the class. We walked to the window and looked out. We stared at the mottled leaden sky, the little mounds of rubble in the rutted, empty streets.

'You also have the right to close your eyes,' Sarah Kwong informed us.

I closed my eyes, the scenery changed or didn't, sometimes we stood by an equatorial river, sometimes we were alien to everything forever, sometimes we writhed lugubriously beyond the edge of death. The exercise consisted in coming back to face Sarah Kwong and ask questions, or answer them.

'Where are we?' I asked.

Sarah Kwong waited for my question to stop echoing off the walls. Then she answered:

'Inside my dreams, Dondog, that's where.'

There was something unambiguously cold in her voice, and she shot me an unpedagogical glance, a negating glance, as if my being had lost all significance, or as if my reality were only the most gruesome of hypotheses.

That was what I didn't like about school, seeing all my certainties about everything demolished with such self-assurance.

Sarah Kwong added:

'And when I say my dreams, I am not thinking of yours, Dondog. I am thinking of mine, Sarah Kwong's, and no one else's.'

Sentences like that didn't do much to change my mind about school.

25

Wulf Ogoïne

While we're recalling events of the distant past, we may as well regress all the way back to the primal time, whose images always come to me when I go rummaging in some corner of my memory. Alas, the images are very clear, as clear as if it were yesterday. It was amid fear and chaos that I came into this world, it was surrounded by a circle of howling old women that I came to be, and when I speak of coming into the world or coming to be I do not use the words lightly, this is my own birth and no one else's, and from that day forward, a date that I myself mark with a black stone, everything began to go wrong for me, not always completely wrong, to be sure, and sometimes less disastrously wrong than others, but all the same wrong on the whole, on an arc forever sloping toward degeneration and failure, in the end leading me to this second circle of babbling old women, completing the circuit, in the end leading me to a tedious trial judged by my entire community of grandmothers, during which I embraced the terms of my accusation with all the power of my remorse, my indictments ever more damning with each passing month and each passing season, until at last I was given a sentence of death without possibility of appeal, immediately followed by an execution that seemed anything but a charade, but that nevertheless, as we have seen, the old women proved unable to make good. I was hoping to be rid at last of the burden of life, to be honorably riddled with bullets before the ewes and camels, in a place where crushing abstractions, a crushing sky and sparse pastures, are all that remains of the earth. I was hoping to leave this life on a note of something other than failure, but long ago it was ordained that I would never be granted the beginning or end I might by rights expect. This was not a new thing: from the first second of my awakening, that same frustrating phenomenon has accompanied my every step. Take for instance my eruption from unconsciousness. Without transition, I left the latent state that so pleasantly follows nonexistence, and fell straight into the turbulence that, over a lifetime, so horribly and tediously precedes death. They call that awakening, that passage from one state to another. It took place against a sonic backdrop of lugubrious cries intoned by my seventeen or twenty-nine or forty-nine grandmothers, meant to make a mind flicker on inside me, meant to make me begin writhing in the manner of living things, and then hurtle at once down the path they'd planned out for me. And when I say lugubrious cries I don't mean it as a joke: even today, every memory of those rhythmic howls and incantations covers me with clamminess and new excrescences. As one, my progenetrixes panted out a succession of strident threnodies over a sepulchral bass chorus; Laetitia Scheidmann, lost in a shamanistic trance since midnight, beat on a tambourine decorated with bells and rattles shaped like yak-headed mares or young sorceresses or bears. Solange Bud and Magda Tetschke danced beside her, and a half-dozen others as well, but it's those two I see most clearly. With supernatural strength they dragged me out of the twelve pillows among which I'd been scattered to elude the weekly searches, and from the void they extricated my head, my meaty and meatless parts, my viscera, all the while squeezing my brain to be sure it was ripe, to be sure it would serve their purpose without faltering. It was eight o'clock in the morning. The birthing dance had gone on all night long. The Olmès sisters' needlework had striated me with seams and scars that branched off into my soft entrails and pockets of organic matter, all the way down to my hard bones. Their stitchwork had strewn my skin with pinpoints of acidic fire that did not mend, but on the contrary began to gnaw into my depths. Although not yet fully awake, I dimly realized that my flesh would bring me suffering in the near future. The deep, tuneless notes sounded by a wriggling Solange Bud and Magda Tetschke, or Sabiha Pellegrini or Varvalia Lodenko, were beginning to fracture various sticky husks and hulls deep inside me, beneath which my death lay protected, perfectly innocuous, preserving the absolute zero of my existence, and, let us note, doing no harm within me or anywhere else. But already Sabiha Pellegrini had thrust her right hand into my thoracic cavity, as Mongols do when they want a beast to stop living and become food, and now her hand crept onward; she sank her nails into the approximate location of my death, adroitly feeling her way around the darkest of obstacles, and her hooked fingers drew nearer to my death, preparing to give it the sharp pinch that would snuff it out at last. Suddenly, and this marked the end of my stay in the darkness, where I had so long lain in perfect contentment, suddenly light burst forth inside my skull, and I felt the unbearable burning of my first sigh. 'It's coming, he's coming!' someone growled. The shamanic percussion doubled in intensity. A fetid gas snaked through my lungs, ravaging the alveoli, a thousand embers blazed in my bronchial tubes. I opened my eyes and experienced my first images. Gowns and multicolored felt bonnets swooped and billowed above me, old women of inconceivable age clutched at me and shook me from my apnea, singing frightening songs and dancing frightful dances, my grandmother Laetitia Scheidmann ululating like a madwoman, my grandmother Solange Bud trumpeting syllables from beyond the grave, my grandmother Magda Tetschke reaching out toward me and howling. Judging that the moment had come, Varvalia Lodenko launched into a long recitation of the tasks I would have to accomplish to rescue our egalitarian society and to bring together in brotherhood all the scattered debris of human beggary still wandering the planet. I pushed out the loathsome air, longing for the void, already seeking some way back into the serenity of the void, but life was now upon me, manipulating my lungs, inflating me once again in spite of myself. Unbearable pain and fear. That's what comes into my mind when I'm asked to travel back to the furthest edge of my memories, or when, for instance, you ask me to explain the nostalgia for a black paradise that follows me everywhere and never lets go, and that always, at one time or another, visits those who move and speak in the space of my strange narracts. I was born against my will, you confiscated my nonexistence, and for that I reproach you. My awakening was a nightmare, and that's another reason for my ill humor. I don't like hearing Laetitia Scheidmann's drum again, and seeing Solange Bud and Magda Tetschke beside her again, her camp-mates and eternal accomplices, dancing to a complex rhythm, now in seven beats, now two, now thirteen, their bodies rising like birds mimicking other, much heavier birds, or like angels displaying their fall in a final attempt to earn their fellows' respect. That's where I come from, from that savage ceremony. These deathless women gave me life; I owe them everything, and I can't imagine being so ungrateful as to forget it, and when I say these women I am thinking of you, of course, who turned your rifles against me and didn't riddle me with bullets. Nevertheless, whatever my debt to them might be, I cannot forgive you that originary minute, nor can I forgive the destiny you despotically laid out for me, when all I asked was to sleep uneventfully where I lay, which is to say nowhere. With no joy whatsoever I remember that first second, that first minute. I sat up on my rump, tormented by a terrible itch, feeling as though I were on fire. My skin seemed something separate from me, some grotesquely ill-fitting sort of container. I thought I could feel my dermis flapping about me in half-stitched banners, limp tatters, horrible, tender fringes. You were dressed for the occasion in your finest embroidered clothes, you'd dug into your trunks for ancient wedding gowns and old mourning robes, their rotting sleeves fallen away a hundred years before, and I imagined my skin not only writhing around and apart from me but also organically melded with those fabrics, whose smell of yak fat and nomadic grime now flooded my nostrils and filled me with despair. I sensed that the physical boundary between me and you had not been established and never would be, that I was only an outcropping from your physical totality, from your collective being, and that soon, which is to say when my life came to an end, I would be rejoined with your mass, and lose myself within it. At this prospect I let out a howl of terror, but you paid no mind; now that I think of it, my voice might not yet have had force enough to reach your ears. 'It's coming,' someone said. 'He's going to cry in a moment! . . . It's coming, it's coming! . . . Drum louder! . . . Don't stop drumming! . . .' When I say someone, I don't know who I mean, I only know that it wasn't Varvalia Lodenko, since she was at that moment pouring political teachings into my fontanelles, to complement and complete the messages already many times engraved into the waxy paste of my intelligence, which now had to be magically activated so that with my first autonomous movements I would be shunted onto the track you'd laid down for me. After a half-minute, other immortal centenarians came along to back up Varvalia Lodenko, other overseers of ideology. Katharina Zemlinski was there, and Esther Wundersee, Eliana Badraf, Bruna Epstein, Gabriella Cheung, and a dozen more grandmothers of the same stripe. A fearsome tumult filtered into me through the various bony labyrinths implanted inside my skull. From this emerged something ordered, a coherent discourse, the old women's rasping voices once again delivering an account of the society that their generation had built and buttressed all over the planet, that they'd rescued with admirable self-abnegation in its hours of need, such that in the end even the ruins could no longer hold up. A dense arch took shape over me, formed of warm breath and arthritic hands and coarse, rutted faces. The intermingled fabrics whirled this way and that, the dust wheeled from one mouth to the other. Their words described the state of things after and before the world revolution, pelting me like falling hail. I took all this in, all these sentences, all those gutturals recounting a universal disaster, and, second by second, my understanding of the situation grew. In truth, my grandmothers were only repeating the words they'd spoken over me all through my gestation, as I lay in pieces, inert in the old beds of the dormitory or between mattress and springs or deep in the secret confines of eiderdowns or pillowcases. Now their teachings settled over me in enormous heaps, and I assimilated them automatically, with no need for reflection. Instantly I understood the instructions those voices dictated, and the numbers by which they portrayed the state of the world. The overview was of a sort to vanquish all hope. Humankind was now nothing more than a handful of scattered particles, rarely colliding. The survivors felt their way through the twilight without conviction, unable to distinguish their own individual unhappiness from the wreckage of the collectivity, seeing, like me, no difference between the real and the imaginary, confusing the lingering evils of the old capitalist system with the drift and decline of the non-functional non-capitalist system. Onto my shoulders the old women insistently placed the future of the world, or at least of its axis, for all the days to come. My task was to shake myself off and speed away from the home, avoiding every checkpoint, to race through the taiga to the capital and begin the elimination of the guilty, of the last men still holding power — even if it meant shortening them by a head, Varvalia Lodenko insisted — after which I was expected to find some way to escalate the revolution until some kind of dynamic was restored. This was what they asked of me, before the last debris of humanity were reduced to impalpable powder. I struggled to my feet, feeling the old women's shamanic hands upon me. Their shamanic fingers vigorously worked all that remained indefinite inside me; I needed a childhood, and they made me an ersatz childhood, I needed a carefree youth and dreams, and these they transmitted with magical brayings of terrifying density, each bray equaling two thousand four hundred and one images of dreams and three hundred forty-three days of carefree frolic. The shamanic fabrics called up memories of rancid butter and churned tea, of female yak teats and penniless nomadism, and I sneezed. That sound set off a wave of joy: it proclaimed that I was now an autonomous individual. I hurled myself toward the window, plowing through the assembly of overwrought ancestors as they bellowed farewells and revolutionary slogans. I brushed past felt vests, trousers of Mongolian silk, your wrinkled faces, toothless down to the collarbones, suddenly ecstatic to see me on my feet, confident of the future, and also, I can say this today, looking back, suddenly glorious. Picking up speed, I obeyed your urgings and flung myself out the window, landing on the grassy expanse before the watchtowers and the first larches. Oncoming bees lashed my face, along with a few dragonflies and horseflies, and at the same time I grievously toppled a figure who stood in my way, no doubt Tarass Brock, the nuclear maintenance engineer, who'd picked the wrong day to come and murmur sweet nothings into Rosa Matrossian's ear, and then I began galloping toward the northwest, where you told me I'd find the capital. I plunged into the woods, into the brush rich in red cranberries and fox droppings, or squirrel droppings, down trails haunted only by bears, deep in the old impenetrable forest whose giants go on standing for a hundred years after their death. I found peace in my speed and my solitude. It was already nine-thirty in the morning. I ran without pause, never breathing more than necessary, so as not to become drunk on the pine resin, to ward off all thoughts of surrender, to help myself resist the politically unfruitful lures of a hermit's life in the taiga. In short, I obediently observed your every precept in those moments that followed the real beginning. I never relaxed my gait, night or day. I measured the passing time by units of twelve full moons. The taiga was deserted, more and more frequently broken by clearings that sometimes stretched for thousands of kilometers. Roads and urban centers began to multiply. In most of these cities a handful of ruined men and women could be found, lying slack in deep spiritual lethargy, but in general, there was no one. The streets struck me with their silence, the houses stood in rows, empty, the vagabonds stuck close to their hiding places and never answered my calls. Let's summarize all this in our own language by saying that the masses never showed up. They'd all disappeared. The bipedal featherless population had faded into nothingness. I remained in telephone contact with my grandmothers. They'd taken up arms again, and now formed a steely militia that scoured the lands from Kolmogorovo to Vancouver, striving to recreate some political morality among the clusters of humanity spared by the nothingness; but, having met no one on whom to exert their vigilance, they now thought of visiting the capital to admire the changes brought about by my reforms. I did my best to dissuade them, and it was then that they learned I'd reestablished the capitalist system; thus, that day, they announced the opening of disciplinary procedures against me, vowing to expose me to the full fury of a popular tribunal, and then they slammed down the phone. Some of them had been euthanized after the uprising at Spotted Wheat. The others fled endlessly across the empty continents whose geographical or social profiles none of them could now distinguish. One faction, led by Laetitia Scheidmann, set out for the capital to capture me. The others set up camp in the spot designated for the trial, not far from the center of the world, in the environs of Lake Hövsgöl. Awaiting the hypothetical arrival of the penitentiary convoy dispatched by my grandmothers, I took stock of the preceding decades, and of my own actions. I'd had no trouble climbing up through the ranks to the highest offices. Since by this time there was absolutely nothing functioning anywhere, the ambitious had gradually lost their taste for competition, and even the incompetents had wearied of administrative honors and medals. Apathy had descended over the directorial realm, and I had only to open a door and sit down to seize hold of what was once known as power. These were the circumstances in which I signed the decrees reestablishing private property and the exploitation of man by man, and other mafiogenetic abominations that I thought likely to restart the machinery of collective existence and rekindle a permanent revolution. Here, once again, I must acknowledge that this was a foolhardy venture, and that my decrees had the most disastrous consequences. I have little more to say of my life in the capital. At one point, a dog came and rubbed against my legs, an affectionate creature answering to the name Wulf Ogoïne. We remained friends all through the morass that followed the signing of the decrees, and when I say morass I do not use the term lightly, for the rehabilitation of the market economy, which was an odiously brash and pointless pursuit, and which I hoped might at least put certain sectors back on their feet, was accompanied by no improvement whatsoever for anyone. Wulf Ogoïne had coarse fur, an intelligent gaze, and, despite the slight curve of his spine, the air of a peaceable mongrel sheepdog. Every evening we strolled to an esplanade that we'd cleared of rubble, and together we watched the sunset when the sun was shining, or else we stood listening, straining to make out the sound of capitalism reorganizing its mercantile networks throughout the capital. I remember Wulf Ogoïne's way of sniffing disdainfully at the books I read as we looked over the empty city, or the scraps of paper on which I pointlessly calculated the time I'd lived before my birth and the time I had left to live. I remember his piercing bark, his white teeth, his smell in the summer, his smell in the winter. According to my calculations, I'd existed in darkness for twenty billion years, and I'm now forty-eight, and I had, all in all, one single friend, that Wulf Ogoïne. He went away when Laetitia Scheidmann burst into my hovel to clasp the handcuffs over my wrists. I don't know where he might have gone, maybe off to lead a solitary life in the Kanal neighborhood or elsewhere. I don't know if I'll ever return to the black existence I once knew, or if I'll be forcibly stuffed into something else, and, once crammed into that something else, I don't know if I'll ever have a chance to be with my friend Wulf Ogoïne again.

26

Yasar Dondog

Or else she who claims to be a psychotherapist leaves Evon Zwogg on his own for hours on end, sitting before a set of eight black-and-white photographs, the same changeless images time after time, which she lays out on the polished tabletop before climbing the stairs to the upper level, where she directs an educational center.

'I'll be back, Zwogg, don't go anywhere,' she says.

From the ceiling comes the sound of her irregular footsteps, of someone moving a cinder block or a crate. Then everything is quiet.

Outside the paneless windows, the city lies still. When the wind blows, streaks of dull red dust drift over the floor like moving veins of red marble, like the landscape on Mars, supposedly. Often the sky seems to lose all its color, washed out by the dazzling sunlight. Clouds of swallows turn dizzying circles between the buildings of the Kanal district. For three quarters of an hour they harass each other, crying shrilly, then all at once they fly off. Silence returns to the room. Evon Zwogg sifts through the photographs. He knows them all by heart, particularly because they're all prints from one single negative, distinguishable only by their varied degrees of contrast. Sometimes, she who claims to heal the insane comes down from upstairs, opens the door, and asks Zwogg if he has anything to say about the photographs. Zwogg shrugs his shoulders. She waits for a minute, then closes the door and heads back upstairs. She's a beautiful woman, beautiful in a quietly celestial way, like so many Chinese women. Her dress is casual, faded jeans, a jean jacket, and a black tee-shirt. Closing the door, she promises to come back soon.

When they aren't being pursued by the swallows, and when the wind isn't howling, dragonflies find their way in through the window. The blazing light of the sun sometimes makes it difficult to admire their beauty. Let's say that they're often blue, a blue tending toward turquoise. Some of them hover tremblingly before Evon Zwogg, and over the photographs. Sometimes, out of boredom, Evon Zwogg catches one and eats it.

A little later that day, I enter the mostly empty room where Evon Zwogg sits daydreaming, and when I say I, I'm thinking mostly of Yasar Dondog, I should make that clear from the start. I sit down beside him in the Martian dust, brick or rust-red, amid the debris of the dragonflies. We introduce ourselves and begin to get acquainted. After a moment, I speak to him of Maggy Kwong.

'The shrink? You live with the shrink?' says Evon Zwogg, stunned.

'No,' I say. 'Not her. That's Sarah Kwong. I live with her sister, Maggy. We sell vegetables at the market.'

Reassured, Evon Zwogg rearranges the photographs that lie waiting before him, then chooses one and presses a sweaty finger against it.

'You see, here, this is the past. That's my grandfather.'

I examine the photograph in my turn. The dog-eared cardboard shows me a snowy landscape, not far from a railway line, and three men, two dressed in civilian rags, the third bundled up in military rags and feebly threatening the others with a knife. It could have been anywhere, at any time.

'Which one?'

'Which one what?' Evon Zwogg says with a start.

'Your grandfather—which of these three is he?'

An outraged look crosses Evon Zwogg's face. He makes a stack of the photographs, turning them over so that I can't see them. His fingers are trembling. I don't know how to repair whatever might be repaired between us.

'And you,' he suddenly says, violently, 'of the two of us, which one are you?'

27

Rita Arsenal

A few facts before the visit begins, a few numerical references. My death dates back a hundred billion years, like everyone else's, and my life forty-eight; as I've already said, here and elsewhere, I don't know if there's an end to all this, or how long I'll have to go on fleeing before I reach that end. More numbers. The pines, larches, and arollas around us attain heights ranging from thirty-four to fifty-seven meters. The anthill before us, which seems deserted but isn't, opens onto a network of underground tunnels with a radius of thirty meters, thanks to which the ants can pass unobserved throughout the entire area of the ruins that concern us today. At this time of year, the temperature in the woods averages twenty-four degrees centigrade, but in winter the readings fall to forty below, with an occasional extreme in the region of minus fifty. There is a crystalline quality to the silence then. The forest seems utterly devoid of life from here to the river, which lies immobilized under the ice for five months of the year. The mammals are not as numerous as they once were, and by once I mean the time of the insurrection's birth. A handful of squirrels frolic high above in the month of July, and sometimes a fox can be seen trotting past, but no species has recovered the genetic richness required to thrive. Since long ago, the only wolves or bears one might encounter here are to be found in dreams. When I say one, I am thinking of no one in particular. Just a bit more numerical background. The insurrection in the nursing home took place two or three hundred years after the world revolution. The building, since vanished, housed some forty aged lodgers, principally female, whose resistance to death was no longer in doubt. Their aptitude for feigning immortality was no longer even a matter of scientific controversy, in part, no doubt, because ninety-five percent of all the researchers were dead. Every year a veterinarian from the capital sent a batch of questionnaires, which the director filled out as best she could. This file was placed in the hands of the postal crew as they passed by, for such a service existed in those days. Among the home's personnel were a director, a forest ranger who shared the director's bed in the winter months, and five housemaids, among whom it is customary to mention a mother and daughter, Ludmilla Matrossian and Rosa Matrossian. The objects preserved from that time are few in number; they bear witness to an autarchic existence in a setting that combined all the advantages of a private retreat and a prison. In addition to furniture and various household articles, the excavations have uncovered a van that the forest ranger once used to patrol the seven kilometers of paved roads surrounding the home. According to legend, this vehicle broke down during a parade commemorating the bicentennial of the Komsomols, an organization greatly esteemed by the old women, and never moved again after that day. The remains of the wreck can be seen, pulled up from below ground by the growth of a giant larch, in the western sector of the site, an area now reclaimed by the forest. More numbers, this time concerning Spotted Wheat's relative geographical isolation. Twenty-two kilometers from here there once stood a deserted experimental farm, with greenhouses powered by nuclear combustion. The farmers abandoned the site when the generator's atomic core began to melt. This enterprise was already closed at the time of the uprising. Only two engineers remained behind, for maintenance purposes: Tarass Brock, a man of fifty-two, and Rita Arsenal, a physicist with a debilitating case of depression, who apparently spent her days sitting on the burning hot concrete of the nuclear basin, listening to the rumble of the fission and murmuring postexotic tales with her eyes closed. Tarass Brock made frequent visits to Spotted Wheat on the pretext of decontamination procedures, but in truth he was only coming to call on Rosa Matrossian. On the day of the uprising, he'd brought her a basket of cranberries in hopes of overcoming her continued resistance to any suggestion of sexual relations. But let us now begin our tour, which consists of four segments, one for each point of the compass. If we wished, we could easily abridge our visit, and see everything from one single fixed point, as for instance from the foot of that pine tree, near the small mound I pointed out a moment ago, and which is nothing other than a giant anthill built around a Geiger counter that once belonged to Tarass Brock. Here we can see a moss-covered protrusion, which proves that we are indeed on the site of the ruins and not somewhere else in the taiga. Let us imagine the facade that once stood on this spot. We have before us the dining hall, the corridor, the kitchen. On the second floor is the dormitory where Will Scheidmann was conceived. With a bit of effort, we can picture Will Scheidmann leaping from a window, landing in a bank of begonias, just where this pine tree has erupted from the ground, then briskly rebounding and beginning his long race toward the northwest, grievously jostling Tarass Brock on the way. In the kitchen, Rosa Matrossian had begun warming the salty tea for breakfast. From one corner of the room the basket of cranberries released its perfume. Tarass Brock had laid out his radiation-measuring devices on the front step, setting them to crackle only in the most extreme circumstances, in the proximity of a nuclear torrent, say, or clasped between Rita Arsenal's arms. The morning was already warm. The environs of the experimental farm had seen a great burgeoning of cicadas, and they had recently invaded this area, manifesting a desire to impose their musical norm upon the world. Nevertheless, that morning's din had nothing to do with mutant insects. It was composed of shamanic brayings intended to help Will Scheidmann extract himself from the void, along with a growing clamor of hand-to-hand combat, for as always the staff was opposing the old women's plan. Here we have the little room that Yaliane Heifetz called the boudoir. Here a television set stood enthroned, having received no signals for sixty years, all broadcasting having long since come to a halt. There, where colossal ferns now tremble, Yaliane Heifetz sat and summoned up her youthful memories, there she recalled anecdotes from her days heading an agency of international struggle against the capitalist system. Rosa Matrossian was cornered in this room, the rug slipped beneath her feet, she caught herself awkwardly on the television stand, the receiver fell and cracked open her skull. Today we have neither the television set nor the carcasses of the couches and armchairs to help us imagine the quiet evenings that passed by in this boudoir. For some time, this area was strewn with rubble left by the collapse of the roof and then of the upper floor, but now it has all disappeared. Rain and melting snow have gradually displaced the vestiges, wind has scattered the essential dusts, moss has blurred the edges of the ruins, several generations of trees have erased their outline. Further on, behind the trunk of that larch, rose the first steps of the staircase down which Ludmilla Matrossian was tossed, and where a nurse's aide soon found herself with a broken neck, like the director who'd climbed the stairs to the dormitory a few moments before. She was greeted by a welcoming committee armed with ritual conches, and a moment later she lay under a bed to the left of the door, in a pool of urine and blood, her legs still twitching. The sound of these skirmishes disturbed the tranquility of the home until about noon that day. Now direct your gaze toward the carpet of moss directly in front of that stump. You will notice a slanting structure that resembles a second anthill. This is in fact a second wall. It was against these bricks that Rita Arsenal collapsed. She'd spent the winter alone, vainly awaiting Tarass Brock's return, and finally she decided to go and look for him at the home. This spot still glows in the dark. Rita Arsenal's death dated back some hundred billion years, like everyone else's, and at that time her life dated back forty-five or forty-six. We do not know where Rita Arsenal might be at present, nor in what state. This concludes our visit.

28

Freek Winslow

We'd been walking for six hundred and eighty nights, and then something changed. The atmosphere wasn't the same. We'd begun to find large pieces of cloth hung across our path. We had to slash our way through with knives, or enlarge the existing rips by hand. Some claimed these were nothing other than spider webs; others held that we were dreaming, and that, if living beings had hung sheets of such considerable size and strength in our path, it was not to entrap us, not even to slow us down, but only to warn them of our approach, to alert them that we would soon be emerging into their reality. 'Hogwash,' retorted our captain, a certain Brickstein. 'We're going through a sail factory,' he asserted, 'an enormous factory, abandoned centuries ago. Those are jibs, topgallants, and mizzens you're slashing.' An odor of salty dust clung to our hands, an odor of mildewed thread, an odor of tar and tarpaulins on our hair and our clothes, an odor of hardtack and torn fabric on our lips. Spreading out to avoid wounding each other, each of us separately hacked at the invisible shrouds and slipped through the holes.

And so we moved forward, feeling our way, our progress endlessly slowed, abrading our hands on the rough folds of cloth, when suddenly, at the heart of the six hundred eighty-sixth day, the watchman announced there was light up ahead. An hour later, our own retinas confirmed this news.

We had passed from absolute darkness to twilight.

Emitting no hurrahs, but with an electricity on the surface of our souls that urged us to conversation and even laughter, we left the sail-works behind us and advanced into the grayness. Soon we came upon a small port village. Only five were left of our group: Jean Brickstein, the captain; Meetraf Vaillant, the watchman; Freek Winslow, the chief boatswain's mate; Nayadja Aghatourane, our shaman; and Khrili Gompo, the traveler.

After a moment we crossed into a blind courtyard, one last corridor of earth, and, since the path ended there, our good humor deserted us. A few remnants of light from the setting sun lent a violet tint to our surroundings. Behind us the landscape was studded with the stumps of collapsed warehouses. We zigzagged our way through the rubble to the edge of the basins, where we wordlessly considered the shattered fishing boats, half-buried in mud for the rest of time. The scene was drenched in horrible colors. The estuary was now only a heartbreaking expanse of mud. In the distance, more than a kilometer away, the lace of the first waves recalled a spray of vomit.

'Salt water at twelve hundred meters,' the watchman estimated.

Forbidding anyone to follow, Freek Winslow ventured out onto the jetty until he came to a break in the stone; unable to advance any further, he retraced his steps.

There was no one to be seen in the port, and no one on the water. The only form we could make out on the horizon was an islet, but the watchman assured us that the islet in question would be gone in a week, once the meat had decomposed and the seagulls and crabs had ripped it apart. 'What meat?' asked Khrili Gompo. On closer inspection, it was indeed a mountain of limp flesh that we'd spied in the distance. A giant squid had run aground on a sandbank, and hadn't had time to protest its own death. For diurnal birds the hour was incongruous, so the gulls had for the moment suspended their assault.

Freek Winslow turned his back to this spectacle and sat down on a mooring post. His eyes were closed. He sat facing the ruins, and through his eyelids he feigned an interest in the darkness, in the way it invaded the empty town.

It was now Freek Winslow that we consulted whenever we had an important decision to make. Our captain's many missteps had cost him his authority; as for Nayadja Aghatourane, the shaman, she could have offered useful counsel, but her innate autism had evolved in the wrong direction, and she was no longer communicative.

After a minute of prostration, Freek Winslow began to speak.

'This whole thing has got off to a bad start,' he said.

We sat down on the rubble. Khrili Gompo was holding his breath. We understood that a day would come when he could no longer delay his disappearance, a day when his dive would come to an end, and he would fade away.

'Our enclosure will drive us insane,' Winslow went on. 'In the conditions that await us, our confinement will soon become nightmarish. The idea of remaining together will weigh heavy on us all. We'll hate that idea so much it will kill us, so much that we'll find ourselves driven to bite and pummel each other. We'll never overcome our aggression, that repugnant urge buried deep inside each of us, that repugnant animal drive to do harm to our fellow man, to defeat him. Imprisoned night and day beneath this hermetic vault, we will lose all our sense of fraternity, and all our refinement.'

He cleared his throat. His prediction terrified us all the more in that we didn't entirely understand it. Was this something imminent he was speaking of, or did it involve only a very distant future?

'In the end, we will come to accept our immense spiritual ugliness,' he added in a murmur. 'It will be horrible.'

After an hour or two, hearing him add nothing further, we went our separate ways.

Once again, darkness enveloped us. There were still five of us, still breathing or holding our breath, each distant enough from the others to resist all temptation to bite, murder, or dismember.

We had no further news of Freek Winslow for several years. From time to time, the wind brought us the cawing of gulls, the stink of rotting sperm whales or squid. Sometimes we woke up, sometimes we went and wandered among the ruins, sometimes nothing happened for months at a time. Winslow's predictions didn't seem to be coming true. We felt oppressed, our enclosure beleaguered and broke us, our refinement had declined, but we waited without violence. Sometimes we gathered near the jetty. We exchanged a handful of sentences, then slipped away toward a still darker place, into our individual shelters, whose location we carefully kept secret. From time to time, a few of us went off in search of a route to the ocean and wound up foundering in the mud, or tried to repair the fishing boats and ended up injured.

In short, then, we resisted all criminal impulses. We now know that Freek Winslow had gone off to work as a bus driver in the next city over. Vaillant, the watchman, recently married a native, and no longer visits the port. Khrili Gompo is nowhere to be seen. Of our captain we learned that he'd taken advantage of the rebirth of capitalism to open a spanker shop, but he has no customers, a fact that he often laments. In our situation, I think it's best not to become too agitated, and simply to wait. When I say I, I am thinking of Nayadja Aghatourane, and when I say wait, I mean with no idea what might come along.

I do not move.

I wait here, facing the ocean, facing what remains of it.

29

Jessie Loo

Once I'd reached my daily quota, I settled back against the cement bleachers of the sports complex and watched a friendly tournament between local basketball teams. Evening was gathering little by little, and the mosquitos mercilessly savaged the players' perspiring flesh, endless waves of commandos landing anywhere there might still be a bit of red to be found. As this was an athletic encounter of no real significance, the floodlights were not lit, and the players were forced to make do with the illumination dispensed by the nearby streetlights. The basketball players toiled in a darkness of increasing density, flailing both to control a ball they could scarcely see and to crush the insects gathering by the dozens to bite them on the nape of the neck or the back of the thigh. I heard the slaps, the players' panting breath, the bouncing of the ball, the metallic echo of the basket when a shot hit its mark, various interjections, some tactical, others lamenting a setback. The players were generally women, and, judging from the phonetics of their shouts, principally Chinese refugees. I could never sit on those hard concrete bleachers for long. Soon I would stand up and lean on the fence. Inevitably, that was when Clara Güdzül appeared, walking past the first row of bleachers, where the players' belongings lay momentarily abandoned. She found her way under the stands, an iron rod in her hand, searching for plastic bottles and aluminum cans that might have escaped my vigilance. These she threw into a bag larger than she was, for later sale to a recycler. This was her livelihood, and mine too, since nowadays the capitalist system offered us only private initiative and individual advancement, and no longer the pension and the rest home we'd always thought would be ours. Clara Güdzül rummaged patiently with her stick, carelessly throwing herself down on all fours to retrieve her booty, perfectly impermeable to any onlooker's gaze, or any rat's or spider's, and then she set off again, tiny, dark, grumbling, her back badly stooped. The match continued behind us, but most often I would make up my mind to follow her, dragging my own clattering bag behind me. There was nothing to bind me to the Chinese basketball players, whereas Clara Güdzül and I were linked by a shared old-folks destiny. And so we walked on for a few hectometers, the disagreeable ruckus of the bags at our heels, never exchanging a word, aware of each other's nearness, of course, but with nothing in particular to say. Soon we would be past the streets yellowed by the so-called urban illumination, and back in our neighborhoods of choice, which is to say, of disaster.

This time, Clara had been walking ahead of me for more than a half-hour, with an old woman's scurrying gait, handicapped by the nocturnal heat and the iron rod slung like a rifle over her chest. She spotted a pay telephone across a puddle swollen by the rains of the week before, its surface covered with duckweeds. For the moment, their green was eclipsed by the darkness, but if you were to see them by daylight you would find them a moving sight, and when I say you I am thinking mostly of myself, which is to say Jessie Loo. Disturbed by the sound of our footsteps, a garter snake wriggled into the mud, putting a hole in the layer of vegetation; inside, the water was fantastically black. The old woman made her way around the puddle. She was barefoot. The air smelled of mildewed cinnamon, rubbery stagnation, orchids: very intoxicating odors, the kind you never tire of. Moths skimmed over the surface of things, colorless in the dark, but possibly white or orange, flying low over the flooded pavement, the palms at the end of the street, the taxis waiting outside the telegraph building, or maybe vermilion in spite of the dark, or crimson, or oil-blue. Clara Güdzül walked among them. She gripped the wooden uprights of the frame that supported the telephone, and pulled herself up to the receiver. Her body was shrunken, shorter than her spike; her gaudy dress hung limp over the damp grass, the belt that should have cinched it now cinched nothing, contained nothing, her fading crone's body lay exposed between two folds of cloth, her breasts like withered peppers. I'd lost the litheness of my younger days myself, the fine figure I once cut, and now people drifted past me, never seeing me. When I say people, I'm thinking of no one in particular, because there was no one much on the sidewalk, apart from the moths, which displayed no identifiable personality. Clara Güdzül dialed 886, then settled down to drowse as she waited to be connected. I squatted on the other side of the phone. Clara Güdzül heard me, she heard breathing on the other end of the line, but, not having spoken for some time, it took her a moment to put together a sentence.

'Let me speak to Varvalia Lodenko,' she finally said.

'For what reason, please?' I asked, disguising my voice.

'This is Clara Güdzül,' she said. 'I'd like instructions for the years to come, that's all.'

'This is Varvalia Lodenko,' I lied. 'I'm glad you called, Clara.'

'Is that you, Varvalia?' she said with some excitement. 'I'm so happy to hear your voice.'

'Where are you?' I asked.

'I don't know,' she answered. 'Seven or eight years ago, I was somewhere around Luang Prabang, but I've walked a long way since then.'

'Luang Prabang,' I sighed. 'Has the capitalist system taken over there, too?'

'I don't know,' she said. 'There's almost no one left anywhere. There are still a few houses standing, a few temples on the river-banks. There's a basketball team.'

'What about capitalists?' I asked. 'What about rich people?'

'I don't know,' said Clara Güdzül. 'I'd love to eliminate some, but I never meet any.'

'If you do, kill them,' I said. 'Get the basketball players to help you.'

'I never meet any,' she insisted. 'I never meet anyone anywhere.'

30

Clara Güdzül

The bottles and cans lie piled in the recycler's courtyard, two pyramids of an almost uniform blue in the darkness. The piles are unstable, and continually disturbed by one animal or another, a rat or a dog in search of some sugar, or sometimes a monkey, a macaque, just as mangy, just as emaciated. A sound of furtive rummaging comes out of the darkness; suddenly the cans go tumbling in every direction, and something runs fleeing into the night. Once the pile falls silent again, the insects in the banana trees resume their nocturnal refrain, a screeching howl that would force you to raise your voice if you had anything to say. But what conversation could you hope to make now, and when I say you here I am more or less thinking of Clara Güdzül, emerging from the darkness, as she does every night, with her trash bag jangling behind her, her rifle-like rod, her curved Untermensch spine, her air of squalid immortality. What sentences could she possibly speak, and to whom? What fragments of an answer could she possibly expect, and from whom?

Now here is Clara Güdzül under the ghastly light, weighing the day's haul, then sorting it, because the rule says you've got to separate your plastic from your aluminum. This you refers far less to Clara Güdzül than the one before, obviously. Then she receives her due, her dollars, money having been reintroduced into society along with the principle of commerce. Two dollars is her usual take.

'I'm rounding up, seeing as it's you,' says the recycler.

Clara Güdzül stuffs the soiled bills under her arm, into a pouch she keeps hidden there, then once again she hitches up her metal rod and sets off. Grumbling or silent, depending on her mood, she withdraws from the circle of light.

She dissolves into the street.

She is no longer there.

Hanging at the entrance to the shop, an acetylene lamp shines over the scales, the counter, the recycler's embittered face, his alcoholic low-income mug, and, in front of the counter, the floor strewn with bottle caps, various rags, and rust, as the recycler also deals in old paper and scrap-metal.

Sometimes, when he doesn't have enough in his cash drawer to pay his suppliers, and when I speak of suppliers I am thinking essentially of myself and Clara Güdzül, the recycler pays them in refuse, rummaging through his pile of trash. Instead of the usual two dollars, he gives them one of the plastic bottles we've just picked up, adding four or five magazines from a stack.

'There you go,' he says. 'The fifth one's a bonus. Very nice, that one, full color.'

Clara Güdzül does not protest, she knows there's no arguing with the ways of the capitalists, she knows she'll just have to wait for the day of the uprising, when we'll all finally have our chance to kill the ones who wronged us, and she returns to the shadows.

Under the towering trees, she follows the sodden pathways, she shuffles toward the river for a quarter of an hour, assailed by the mosquitos, moving ever onward through the chattering night, through the expanding perfumes of the night, and at last she comes to what she calls her home, a straw mattress protected from rain and misfortune by the leaves of a banana tree, a square of dry ground with a small stock of kindling. She sits down and rests, breathing in regular little puffs. She doesn't sleep. Sleep abandoned her after she'd blown out her two hundred fifty-nine candles, and now she no longer misses it.

She waits for the moon to rise over the river and glimmer on the waters she sees through the tree trunks.

When the moonlight is bright she reaches for the old magazines that represent her day's wages and begins to page through them. These publications could have met with great success if humanity weren't in the process of fading away. They're put out by the mafia, and full of photos of naked girls, of young women opening their thighs to the lens and even spreading the lips of their vulvas, just in case people might wish to see even more. With fascinated tenderness, Clara Güdzül contemplates these uncensored anatomical details. It was long, long ago that she forgot what she herself looked like dressed or naked. She presumes that, in one way or another, her body has preserved the form of those here exposed, that it has retained the intimate bulges and ruts here exposed. She returns these smiling girls' unsmiling gaze, she reaches out to their prostituted docility, she asks if the mafia hurt them, if posing hurt them, and how many dollars they were given, and if they know it was Will Scheidmann who brought about the return of the market society, and if the name Varvalia Lodenko means anything to them. She chooses her words carefully, taking pains not to wound the young women. Today, she supposes, they must be utterly ruined or dead.

The moon shines on the river, the night shines, dogs are barking near the dock, Clara Güdzül speaks with the naked girls, she points out a mole here or there that they really should keep an eye on, she tells them she sees a veil of weariness in their eyes, she assures them that she will come back, that we will come back and overthrow the dollar system again, she shows them her rifle leaning against a palm tree, and says: 'I promise you'll have a chance to shoot Will Scheidmann and the mafiosi yourselves, if that's any consolation, if you can't think of anything else to do about all this.' Then she tells them: 'In any case, I'll send you a cassette of Varvalia Lodenko explaining what's to be done when there's nothing more to be done.'

31

Julie Rorschach

Djimmy Iougriev arises, a parvenu of the new era, and for him as for the rest of the world the day has got off to a bad start, a dust-gale is blowing outside, a fine hail submerging the capital, as sandstorms submerged desert villages in the days of the oases, before the dunes crawled from their burning beds to slither over once-fertile lands and choke them into acceptance of nothingness's unsparing dominion, in the days when the words printed on maps still had meaning—let us cite, for instance, for the beauty of the names, Ontario, Dakota, Michigan, Chukotka, Buryatia, Laos—in the days of the old market society, the old dollars, the old camps, and today it is the capital's turn to feel the wind, the breath of the dying earth hisses over the houses, and when Djimmy Iougriev enters the bathroom, where, in spite of the apartment's opulence, no pane of glass protects him from the world outside, the sand stings his hands and face, and he stands in a stupor, distressed by the friability of matter, glimpsing the fragility of his own existence behind it, and then he peers out the little window that looks toward the west, of the city he sees only moving streaks of Martian sand, brick red, red ocher, and, closing his eyes and coughing, for tiny particles of stone have slipped into his throat and under his eyelids, he turns the tap on the sink and nothing flows forth, and he mutters a few words about the bad start his day has got off to, and his mind begins to work with that idea of a beginning, suddenly recalling the impressions occupying his thoughts when he woke, when he ceased to be asleep, hearing the patter of sand on glass, for like many nouveaux riches he had managed to get hold of windowpanes for his bedroom, and he remembers that brief wavering moment as the dream he'd been having faded from his mind, but now he rediscovers that dream's final image or rather its final sequence, startlingly clear now, oppressive, surely presaging something horrible, he's standing on the terrace of a sordid bungalow sheltering from a pouring rain, speaking to a woman who makes no reply, and yet he knows her name, and yet he calls her by name, Julie Rorschach, she's been sharing his body and his destiny since the beginning of the dream, sixty-eight years before, he's been at her side day and night, he's seen her reason falter, but now she never answers him, her madness has deepened, perhaps she's chosen to let herself slip into aphasia, and rather than converse with him she stares at the tropical lawn before them, the very beautiful, violently green grass, she gazes lovingly at two elephants that have happened along and now stand facing them, crosshatched by the rain, their outlines faintly blurred in the downpour, swinging their trunks, sometimes hoisting them over their skulls and shaking their heads, and now, all at once, an odious aspect of this scene is revealed, the elephants' faces are horribly wounded, washed by the torrential rain, I don't think face is too strong a word when one feels a profound sympathy for these beasts, as I do, and when I say I here, I am thinking as much of Julie Rorschach as of myself, the gouts of rain wash the bleeding wounds, the skin has been slashed to form four square flaps, from the top of the trunk to the hairy bumps on their skulls, lazily and partially swinging open with every move of the elephants' heads, a half of one cheek opens up, say, then the mighty slab of skin slaps back into place, and then the animal shakes itself again, his companion does likewise, the trunks twist up toward the heavens and fall again, the ears sway back and forth, once again the flaps gape open and slam shut, their eyes express prayers or passions in a language that no one understands, the deluge washes away the blood, carries away the rivers of blood, diluting its color, such were the images in Djimmy Iougriev's mind when he became aware of the sand blowing on the windowpanes, now suddenly flooding back into his memory, an ugly nightmare, a bad day, portending the worst, he stops coughing and stands petrified before the tap, from which not a single drop flows, then he urinates into the sand-choked sink, and now he's returning to the bedroom, bathed in Martian hues by the light from outside, his gaze wandering over the bed where a woman lies outstretched, not sleeping, his wife, Irma Iougrieva, and to this woman he says, 'I had a terrible dream,' and she cuts him off with an irritable gesture, she doesn't like him forcing his visions on her first thing in the morning, and he falls silent, and in the room next door the children are making a ruckus, the wind always excites them, they know they won't be going anywhere today, the desolated-planet smell leads them into strange behaviors, soon they'll be amusing themselves by speaking in languages no one knows, or extracting brass horns or idiotic electronic games from their cases, they'll open none of the books that the children of the nouveaux-riches should read, and Djimmy Iougriev senses that he will shortly enter the children's room and be angry, that he will reproach them for their absence of interest in anything, for their shameful lack of culture, and for the sluggish faintheartedness whose display he particularly loathes, and now the children have inserted a vocal roll into the clasps of a phonogram, and through the wall he hears the voice of a fashionable singer mimicking one of the immortal Varvalia Lodenko's rhythmic harangues, with all egalitarian content censored out, of course, and Djimmy Iougriev remembers Julie Rorschach and their life together, and he regrets that it's only the voice and music of Varvalia Lodenko that have burst into the apartment, he regrets it bitterly, because deep down he's always longed for the day when Varvalia Lodenko's Martian-red hordes would spray the ruins with machine-gun fire and lay waste to the nouveaux-riches until there was nothing and no one left moving, and until he, Djimmy Iougriev, could rest peacefully with the woman he loves, Julie Rorschach, and melt with her into the elephants and into love, waiting for her schizophrenia to scar over. No question about it, the day had got off to a very bad start.

32

Armanda Ichkouat

The ropes that bound him to the execution post had rotted, and from time to time Will Scheidmann tested their resistance, after delivering a strange narract, say, or at night, when the temperature fell below zero. Then one day the knots finally went limp, and suddenly everything gave way behind his waist.

The old women still had him in their sights, as they had continuously for two years, ever since that first failed volley of shots. They lay outstretched near the yurts, their rifles trained on his person. Laetitia Scheidmann narrowed the wrinkled slits of her eyes; nestling her rifle against her shoulder, she shouted that Scheidmann's ropes had broken, provoking a sudden flurry of activity. Solange Bud raised her rifle in a hostile manner, but still the old women made no move to fire.

Scheidmann freed his hands and stood still beside the post, thoughtful in the whistling wind. He seemed to know nothing of the art of the getaway. Letting the wind ruffle over him, he gazed at the roiling sky and the autumnal birds, the steppe swallows pirouetting in the turbulent air. When I speak of the swallows I am thinking mostly of one among them, by the name of Armanda Ichkouat.

Scheidmann made no attempt to turn this situation to his advantage. His physiology had undergone metamorphoses likely to complicate a headlong flight. Under the effect of the radioactive winter mists, his long scales of sick skin had grown into imposing strips of wrack. Seen from afar, Scheidmann looked not unlike a pile of seaweed atop which a head had been set out to dry. He continued to mumble strange narracts, proving that he was holding himself in an intermediary state between life and death, albeit without any veritable animal substance or real physiological requirements. 'That Scheidmann isn't shootable anymore,' the aged women often said amongst themselves. 'He's turned himself into some sort of narract-making accordion, so what's the point of filling him full of hot lead?'

By this time he had nothing in common with the grandson they'd condemned to death, and they were charmed by the stories he murmured. 'What's the point of attacking something that charms us?' they said, still reaching no conclusion.

And so the old woman lay in the dwarf rhubarbs and the sparse tufts of karagana and the camel dung and yak droppings. Still cradling their rifles, they smoked in silence, as they always did when they had an important decision to make.

Armanda Ichkouat saw Lilly Young arise, and I say Armanda Ichkouat so as not to be forever using the first person, and I heard her volunteer to inform Scheidmann that he was now free to come and go as he pleased. 'I'll go and lay out our conditions,' she said, 'for example that he go on supplying us with strange narracts, but that he'll still be forbidden to enter all regions inhabited by anyone other than us, to keep him from fraternizing with capitalists and enemies of the people.'

Yaliane Heifetz said: 'Here we go, Lilly's off again,' and then someone chuckled, saying, 'We'll never stop her now,' and a third old woman, Laetitia Scheidmann I think, took the pipe from her mouth and concurred: 'It's true, once she gets started, there's no shutting her up.'

Armanda Ichkouat went and flew over Scheidmann, who was recounting these events in his own fashion. I began to repeat his murmur after him, with a delay of one or two syllables. His first person referred not to me, but to himself.

'Their parley goes on,' he was saying, 'and goes on without end. So alike are their shriveled masks that they can only be distinguished by their headgear, for example a simple felt toque for Magda Tetschke, a headband with partridge quills for Solange Bud, or by the embroideries replacing the failing skin on one or the other's cheeks, sometimes emerald green, sometimes ultramarine. The weather's turned foul, they head off toward the yurts, leaving me alone in the downpour, but the rain lets up almost at once, and they go off to tend to their flock, then they lie down once again in the damp grass, and then the water freezes, night has fallen, a cold late-October night, then in the morning the sun laboriously dissolves the puddles' icy shells, then once again come the dusk and the glacial night. The moon is in its first quarter. Then everything speeds up again and, while the old women struggle to decide whether they will or will not finish me off before springtime, a series of days and nights goes by, and finally the moon is in its last quarter. Then the sun makes a brief appearance, the west goes dim, the night comes. The next day passes, the weeks go by. Never more than one narract every twenty-four hours, no matter how often they ask. December, January. Snowstorms, the steppe blinding by day, horribly white and brilliant under the stars by night. By turns, the old women go off to warm themselves. Now and then a red bonnet or a tuft of feathers takes a practice shot, and a bullet comes whistling into the post near my head. The odor of milky tea wafts toward me, the odor of dung-fueled flames, the odor of felt overcoats. No more than one strange narract per day, on that point I remain firm, but, if anyone wants to know, I'm glad to be with my grandmothers. I'm glad not to be with the capitalists anymore, and to be with my grandmothers again.'

33

Gina Longfellow

Now came the sound of Lilly Young's footsteps, on her way to inform Will Scheidmann of his reprieve. Now came the sound of her little felt boots treading over the white budargana and the violet budargana, their shoots already faded to a uniform gray, falling to dust at the slightest contact. For two years the ground now beneath the tricentenarian's feet had been forbidden to all, even the animals, ever since the elders came forward to ply Will Scheidmann with yogurt liquor, then withdrew to their firing posts. Of this circular patch, far from picturesque, with its tiny green dale and its little dip and its small stones, so familiar to Scheidmann's gaze that he'd ended up giving each one a nickname, of this patch Scheidmann occupied the center, and now that the condemned man had slipped his bonds, the center had become double: there was the post, black and stained, and Scheidmann, two meters away, himself black and stained, and bizarre. Lilly Young approached, creating a third pole, topped with a red bonnet.

She began to perorate. Her speech went on endlessly, as was always the case when Lilly Young took the floor. She hadn't yet finished the harangue, and already the cold of night was blowing, and already the first stars were beginning to shine overhead.

'And then you can put up a yurt somewhere close by,' she was saying, 'or move into Varvalia Lodenko's felt tent, because she's gone away, has our Varvalia, she's gone off to visit the last bastions of civilization, trying to repair your foolishness, and she won't be back anytime soon. And then, when we go back to our nomadic ways, you'll take down your tent and follow us, since we can't let you out of our sight. And if you want a few animals . . .'

Scheidmann paced before her, veering this way and that, clumsily struggling to keep his distance. He took no pleasure in this amnesty, first because he knew he deserved to die, and then because, until the end of time, he would have to be thankful to his grandmothers for not having punctured his flesh. Nor did he appreciate the lack of concision in Lilly Young's words, and also the old woman's breath put him off, with its stench of vomited rhubarb, of camel's milk cheese, of humus, of saliva a thousand times ruminated, of milky tea, of immortality, of camp slang, of fires fueled with yak droppings, of tar-choked pipestems, of herb soups, of smoke.

The darkness gathered, the moon appeared and then set, there remained three more half-hours of darkness, and then the dawn began to ooze from the east, and then once again the day came to an end. Scheidmann lowered his head, like an animal searching for lichen. He raised his eyes, shook his greasy locks, shook the bundles of vesicular strips that were his arms, and this quivering spread to the long ribbons of skin and squamous flesh that hung from his neck, shrouding his torso and legs. He swayed this way and that. Several nights went by. The moon shrank away, leaving only a slender crescent, then snow-clouds howled low over the steppe, without snowfall, and then came a time of very short days, alternating with nights that left the earth shivering and shrunken with cold. The tufts of violet budargana disintegrated in the twilight. Burned by the frost, the white budargana was now no more than a black mat. Then the sun refused to warm the landscape. The stars turned acidic, turned pale, were reborn against the world's velvety darkness, withdrawn into their own cruel sparkling. The diurnal and nocturnal images followed one after another, like slides in a broken projector.

All the while, Lilly Young went on reeling off the terms of the old women's decree, and Scheidmann went on taking a few paces forward or backward, one or two steps left or right, unclear in the shadows, his postures sometimes those of a boxer, sometimes those of a sheep numb with fever. Sometimes Lilly Young sat down cross-legged to rest for a few moments or smoke, or to nibble at a piece of hard cheese drawn from a pocket, or to dismantle and oil her rifle.

Scheidmann had nowhere to go, and, despite the boredom inflicted by Lilly Young's monologue, he did not walk away. To this it must be added that his terror of death had left an exhausting emptiness inside him as it faded. He had difficulty catching his breath, and he abstained from recounting stories of any great length. Two hundred meters away, at the edge of the forbidden circle, Scheidmann's other grandmothers could be seen, equally benumbed by Lilly Young's endless chatter. From time to time one of them felt a part of her intelligence flickering out, and she begged her grandson to pay Lilly Young no mind, and to recite a strange narract. It had been established that the strange narracts flowing from Scheidmann's mouth plugged the leaks in their memory; even if, rather than concrete events, they summoned up dreams or nightmares the old women had once had, this experience of their singing yesterdays helped to stabilize their dying visions. The narracts found their way under their consciousness much like music, by analogy, by polychrony, by magic. That was how they worked.

Thus, that day, Magda Tetschke realized that a chapter of her adventurous youth seemed about to dissolve into nothingness: she had once been in love with Yaldam Reweg, a realist writer married to one of her friends; she'd seduced him and finally married him, and then he was forced to leave, and she'd followed him into deportation. All at once she remembered that friend, of whom she'd heard nothing for two hundred twenty years: Gina Longfellow, who worked beside her at the agency in the days before the world revolution, and who'd remained at her job while she, Magda Tetschke, set out in Reweg's footsteps for virgin lands.

'Hey, Scheidmann!' she shouted. 'Does the name Gina Longfellow mean anything to you?'

Realizing that Scheidmann was not preparing to launch into a narract, she began to crawl toward him. Her rifle moved beneath the moon, among the stalks of dead grass, over the crackling, frost-covered soil. Scheidmann watched as she slowly drew nearer. He didn't know what to say or do. To him, Longfellow was the name of a little stone, next to a pebble he called Reweg. Emerging from her embroidered greatcoat, Magda Tetschke's head swayed back and forth like a turtle's head outside its shell.

'Of course,' Lilly Young continued, 'we don't know when Varvalia Lodenko will be back. But in the meantime you can move into her place. Settle in under her roof, light her stove. There are bricks of dung in the tent, on your right as you enter.'

Now Magda Tetschke was very close. She lifted herself up on her elbows and began to plead in a stentorian voice, begging Scheidmann to whisper her a strange narract, whose principal angel would be Gina Longfellow or Yaldam Reweg or herself, and to make it fast. Seeing him hesitate, she gripped his shoulder and gave him a shake. One of the strips of skin that wreathed Scheidmann came away and stayed in the old woman's hand.

'There, I hope you're happy now,' Scheidmann groaned.

Although it caused him no real pain, this ripping away of his skin filled him with deep disgust.

'Oh, I certainly am,' she said.

She'd backed away a few meters, and now she was rolling over the pebbles, droning out sentences, blissful, raising the half-meter of skin to her nearly blind eyes, trying to read a text in it, imitating a reader's movements in the darkness.

Feigning an eager decipherment of the images inscribed on Scheidmann's strange skin, she mimed a reunion with her friends, her dear friends, and with her memory, all long gone now. And she was happy.

34

Maleeka Bayarlag

The boat had been docked for a week, but the authorization to disembark had yet to be issued. For several days, the indignant passengers raged. They gathered every morning at seven o'clock, scanning the motionless sea, the various structures of the port, and found not a living form to be seen. Then they besieged the commander's cabin, pounding on the thick door armored with copper bands and copper nails, or else they collected their bags and proceeded to the accommodation ladder, vainly attempting to unfurl it and batten it against the hull. The commander refused all communication with them, except by means of notices tacked up in the gangway outside the refectory, between the weather report and the menu. The crew offered outlandish explanations; the officers stalled in response to all questions.

I can't tell you the names of these unhappy passengers. To put it simply, I didn't much mix with them. By nine in the morning they'd scattered through the lower decks, parading their disgruntlement through various hallways and public rooms. Drops of sweat glimmered on their faces, increasingly anxious as the days went by. There were six of them, and then, after a scuffle with the sailors by the ladder, their number fell to four.

There wasn't much light aboard the ship. A warm fog filled the roadstead in the early hours of the day, and a monumental structure towered just beside us, a warehouse several stories high, bathing us in its shadow all day long. The passengers began to complain of this dimness, claiming the gloom caused them psychological distress. They'd stopped changing their clothes and no longer looked after their appearance. Those with a delicate sense of smell began to tense their nostrils whenever they passed by. 'The gringos never wash anymore,' a sailor told me, one of the few who spoke to me, a man from Nazca, in the seaside desert of Peru, where Lydia Mavrani's dreams were often set, back when I was sleeping with Lydia Mavrani, a very long time ago, before we'd lost contact. 'Gringos stink,' he went on, 'and with no soap on their skin they stink even worse.'

Power outages were growing ever more frequent, and in the end the light had to be rationed. Every evening, the crew distributed lanterns with a minuscule supply of oil in their reservoirs. The passengers complained of the smoke from the lanterns and the height of the flame, which consumed their nightly allowance of fuel too quickly for their tastes. Now they were all camped out together in the bar, merging their rants and their animal odors, brandishing glasses in hard-bitten poses, like extras in a bad movie. But the shelves behind the bar were empty, and the drinks they threw back were zero proof. There was nothing on board to be had but warm tea.

The scuffle took place on a Friday; the following Saturday, as a subhuman with some knowledge of shamanism, I was given the task of conveying the bodies ashore, I and the sailor from Nazca and a delegate from the ranks of the passengers who introduced himself as Sheerokee Bayarlag. He'd drawn the short straw. Of him I will spotlight a stunted silhouette, a flat, inexpressive face, almost free of sweat in the early morning, his eyes reduced to deep black slits by their lids. Everyone was wondering if he would take advantage of the situation and head for the hills once he was on land. The captain had instructed us not to give chase, to let him go to his destiny.

We carried the bodies down into the ship's bowels. The holds were hot as ovens. The gringo-hating sailor raised a lantern and explored the metal walls, in search of a numerical reference mark. To our right we saw a series of rectangular hatches, hermetically sealed. Finally the halo of light revealed the marker M891, and a look of relief crossed the sailor's face.

'This is the one,' he said.

For several minutes we clanged at the bolts holding the panel shut. Bayarlag did nothing to help. The opening was just above the waterline, and once we'd pulled away the panel, we were bathed in a milky gleam. The water lay before us, oily and black, with shards of polystyrene floating over the surface. The hole was large enough for our purposes. We had to step over the water, carrying the cadavers on our backs, and grab hold of a rusty ladder that led up to the dock three meters above. The water was calm, and not a wave seemed to be lapping in the dim light.

We'd brought some ropes with us. I won't describe our maneuvers here. Let's just say that the ropes helped us to unload the bodies without dumping them into the water. Sheerokee Bayarlag was the last to set foot on the concrete platform, where we and his companions in sorrow awaited him. He stood before the bodies for fifteen seconds, nervous, unable to collect himself. Now he was perspiring in great drops. We still had to haul our burden to the place the captain had named: behind a vat, fifty meters away. There the dead would lie forever hidden from the gaze of the ship.

Sheerokee Bayarlag said nothing. Staring at the ground, we eyed him surreptitiously, trying to guess when he would finally bolt, zigzagging his way over the deserted esplanade, between the hoists and rusting containers, into the labyrinth of warehouses, where he would easily find cover.

But for the moment he still hadn't bolted, so we dragged the passengers around the back of the vat. The dock was silent, and baking hot. The passengers spread their arms, nodding their heads when they went over a bump. Little mounds of cement dust and dirt piled up under their armpits.

Behind the vat we found a heap of rags and two mattresses,

home to a half-dozen rats and an old beggar woman, so withered that she seemed to have no face. Without protest she watched us lay out the cadavers one meter away, but then she insisted on taking all the dollars we had in our pockets. Sheerokee Bayarlag was the only one of us who'd brought money, no doubt for use in his flight and his new life in a new land. He had two full dollars, and one half. After some hemming and hawing, he dispensed them into the outstretched hand and bent down. He was trembling. Suddenly, as he stood face to face with the old woman, an expression of terrified complicity came over him, as if he'd met her someplace before.

'If you really are Maleeka Bayarlag, tell me my fortune,' he said.

The old woman clutched awkwardly at the coins. One of them rolled toward the edge of the dock and dropped into the water.

'Oh, this isn't my day,' said the old woman.

'Tell me my chances of getting out of this,' Sheerokee Bayarlag insisted.

The old woman raised her faceless eyes to meet his. Sheerokee Bayarlag's teeth were chattering. The old woman was reluctant to speak in our presence. I groaned out a funeral song over the bodies, and then we went away. The old woman was already whispering an oracle, and Sheerokee Bayarlag stood before her, panting and shivering.

We were about to start back down the ladder when Sheerokee Bayarlag emerged from behind the vat and cried out to us. The old woman must have told him this wasn't his day either. He let out a second amorphous cry. We supposed he was terrified that we might leave him stranded here. He shouted again and, since we made no reply, he came trotting to join us.

35

Rachel Carissimi

In the westernmost neighborhood beyond the Rue des Praires, there are cellars where men lock themselves up with dogs and eat them. In the next neighborhood northeast, the mob runs a house where you can learn to kill people with a hammer or a poisoned arrow. Further northwest lie several square kilometers of deserted intersecting streets where no living soul ever wanders. Turning southeast, you come to a neighborhood with eight English refugees and a displaced Cheyenne, along with two Udmurts. Now head south, and you'll find a place where a workers' cooperative once tried to sell the tourists dried fish and carved bones ornamented with slogans and portraits of Communist figures. Of this enterprise nothing remains but a folding metal table and a tourist grown weary of his wanderings, immobile for the past two hundred and eleven years, an imitation-ivory statuette of Dzerjinksi still hanging from his neck. Further south lies a lake whose water is hot in summer and winter alike, and unwholesome. Some people drink it, all the while bemoaning its refusal to cool, even if you leave your container underground for hours. It sparkles repulsively in your mouth. On the eastern shore of this lake lies a barren zone of debris; cut through it, and you'll enter the neighborhood of a shaman known for his unguents, which he uses to reanimate dead squirrels and reawaken dead otters. Once he's revived them, he eats them. On the southern shore stand the remains of a factory whose atomic core has been burning for three hundred sixty-two years. Now make for the southeast, and you'll reach an expanse once occupied by a great train station and several sets of tracks. In a more recently built underground room, you can still see eleven or twelve pairs of rails, running from wall to wall. Behavior-altering gases accumulate beneath the vaulted ceiling. Vagabonds sometimes spend the night in this place; no sooner has the sun gone down than they begin to couple at random, without introductions. Then they eat each other. Further on there are cisterns full of a putrid liquid that some old women use as a shampoo. With this neighborhood behind you, you're within sight of the Rue des Ciels-Chenus. Follow it to the end, and you won't be far from the neighborhood of the Schtern sons, who are fattening up their mother in preparation for eating her. Beyond Ciels-Chenus, over the bridge often called the Buffalo, there is a tiger farm that can only be entered in dreams. The tigers are white and paralyzingly beautiful, and confined under panes of glass set into the ground. They pace back and forth, their heads raised, an impatient tail lashing their flanks, waiting for the glass to break under a passerby's feet. More than one potential visitor is put off by this notion, and in the end few ever come. Advancing northward, you'll notice a stand of trees. There are two willows, one sophora, three aspens, and one elm. Across a half-kilometer of sand you enter a neighborhood where, for two dollars a year, the nouveaux-riches employ a woman to sweep out their rooms and wash their shirts. This woman, Rachel Carissimi, has killed several capitalists, but she didn't eat them. Not far away begins an avenue full of potholes, lined with a string of vacant apartment buildings. In the third building on the odd-numbered side, there nevertheless resides a man who has memorized every one of Varvalia Lodenko's speeches, and can recite them on demand. At the northern end of the avenue, you stand near another cluster of abandoned districts. When I say you, I'm thinking mainly of the Untermenschen, for instance Oulan Raff, which is to say me. Over thousands of hectares a blue-tinged blackish color predominates, and slag, and wind, and, just after that, to the southwest, an expanse of gray tundra opens up before you. If you follow an east-southeasterly course for some three thousand seven hundred kilometers, you will end up at the place known as Spotted Wheat, where a handful of veterinarians once corralled some old women who never died, who never changed, and who couldn't be eaten. The nursing home was far from everything, even the camps. They say these immortals committed a grave error that they never stopped trying to repair. The story goes that they brought a man of rags up out of nothingness, and that he reestablished the circulation of dollars and mafias on the earth. If, instead of choosing that distant destination, you decide to come back toward the Buffalo, you will first enter a courtyard where a windmill wheel squeaks mournfully day and night, connected to nothing. This is where Oulan Raff lives.

36

Adzmund Moïschel

Indefatigably, we put our failures aside and set off once again toward what the maps now showed as blank, yearning to discover if there were still men and women existing in faraway lands, Yorubas or Quechuas or Oroches, and if something still hung in the air over the trenches of Oklahoma, and if a hand might be lent to those taking refuge on the Mekong or the Ussuri or the Pearl River.

One fine morning, our schooner set sail in the solar wind. The wavelets sang their song against the hull, the foresail hummed, and then came a sound of oaths and slapping. The deck was aswarm with flies, disturbing the crew in the midst of their labors. The insects' presence was explained by the buffalo cow we'd taken on to provide us with milk, and later with meat. All manner of things were piled abundantly in the hold, as is usual at the start of a circumnavigation. In addition to sea-biscuits, we'd laid in an immense stock of drinking water, and purification tablets as well, in case our supply was contaminated by miasmas.

We coasted until evening without one loss of human life to mourn; encouraged by this promising figure, we abandoned our plans to drop anchor somewhere for the night, and decided to speed more resolutely southwest. The second mate had just ordered us to unfurl a second sail when the boat hit a mine, abruptly disintegrated, and sank. Down toward the sea floor went our provisions, along with the cow and a dozen men. As fate would have it, the shipwreck occurred only a small distance from shore; the survivors waded back to the beach, happy to be safe but tormented anew by the flies, which had opted not to accompany the livestock to its watery grave.

Once back on dry land, eight sailors demanded to be stricken from the rolls; they set off homeward over the fields. Now we were only nine, little knowing what the next day would bring, and impatient for things to seem clearer in the wake of a good night's sleep. We undressed, hanging our effects on poles to dry, and tried to get some rest, but the insects bedeviled us until dawn. The rays of the sun appeared on the horizon, and none of us had once closed our eyes. Exhausted, we pulled on our uniforms as the other crewmen complained of the health and safety conditions on board. After a violent diatribe from a master rigger named Adzmund Moïschel, they mutinied. The commander was blackjacked; when he emerged from his unconsciousness, his reason had abandoned him. Nearly everyone had deserted. There were only two of us left, including him. We did not go so far as to strip him of his rank, but we relieved him of his responsibilities, which he could no longer perform, as he was babbling prophecy without letup. By we I am here referring principally to myself, as well as the flies, who insisted on taking part in the vote.

Toward noon, we gathered our strength and struck out on a southwesterly course, which is to say in the very direction that had proven so fatal to our craft. A steep embankment ran along the shoreline. Climbing to the top, we discovered a line of tracks and crossties, and began to follow them. The tracks lay some two meters above sea level, hugging the shoreline, which was pocked by a multitude of coves and inlets. Sometimes the rails passed over the water, supported only by concrete pylons sunk into the mud. These spans weren't designed for pedestrians, and we found ourselves forced to hop from tie to tie in a way that soon grew exhausting.

On our left, the deserted moor crackled in the sun. Dogs wandered aimlessly in the distance. They came trotting toward us, and for hours they sniffed at us from afar, barking and hostile. To the right, the shallow waters glimmered. Here and there we saw reed barks beached in the sand, rotting where they lay.

The captain sifted through his interior worlds and spoke to me of his most absurd convictions. 'You know,' he would say to me, 'that Moïschel, I once loved him as people loved their sons, back when they could have sons.' Or else he barked in response to the dogs, or, bitten by a fly, hideously thrust out his lips and buzzed. This was the extent of his conversations' charms.

By four o'clock that afternoon we were within sight of a train station composed of a hut and a siding where a steam locomotive and a tender sat parked, and a tarp-covered platform where travelers might find shelter.

I went to find the man in charge. He was napping in the hut, lulled by static from a radio receiver. No program was airing. He listened to my request for assistance, with no change of expression to foretell his response; then, as dusk was falling, he offered me two mess kits and packets of freeze-dried soup, granting us permission to camp wherever we liked until the next full moon. On that date, he said, the trains would resume their movements, in accordance with the winter schedule.

We settled in under the tarp. The neighborhood was a busy one, and sometimes, delighting in our commander's senseless but entertaining pronouncements, the natives would toss us an offering of food. Not much, but enough to stop us scrabbling through restaurant trash bins and back alleys. A week went by in this way, and then the moon grew fat.

By now the commander had got a grip on his reason, and when the railway workers arrived, he expressed a desire to drive the machine himself; in response, they assured him he wouldn't know how, and, since he refused to back down, the engineer knocked him senseless.

Later he awoke. The convoy was already rolling. Our speed was not great, and our direction was northeasterly. As so often happens, we were heading back where we'd started from. The commander leaned out toward the sea, which now lay on our left. The wind played through his hair, his face bore a triumphant smile. The locomotive whistled every seven seconds; the enormous moon, though still pale, nevertheless draped the landscape in a magical glow. To our right, dogs were running in packs and barking. 'That Adzmund Moïschel, my spiritual son,' the commander shouted, 'how bravely he persisted through every misfortune! . . . Such courage he had! . . . Such intuition! . . . Inverting the compass! . . . Going on ahead of us! . . .'

An intense sensation of joy came over me in my turn. The adventure was finally on again. Southwest or northeast, what does it matter? In bellowing tones, I exhorted the tillerman to hold his course. The land breeze roared in our ears. 'That Adzmund Moïschel! . . .' we exulted in chorus. 'Such courage! . . . Such intuition! . . .'

37

Witold Yanschog

That year, the full moon and the summer solstice coincided again. You'd laid down a number of conditions: the shortest night of the year, a full moon, a Friday, and, to further limit the possibilities, you'd added that a month had to have passed without rain or magnetic storms. The first time, forty-eight years before, all your requirements had been met, but the man never showed up.

That night, you'd sat waiting near the door, on a narrow dune of red sand that obstructed the street, while Alcina Baïadji came and went among the useless implements lined up on cinder blocks, the drum, the herbal garlands, the bottle of perfume, the bottle of lubricant, the bottle of alcohol, and a huge gaudy crown hung with cascading streamers of cloth.

Slowly the moon wheeled over your head. The street was silent. Now and then clucking hens and guinea fowl could be heard from the apartment building, poultry being another of Alcina Baïadji's occupations.

You stared at your feet half sunk into the warm sand, you said nothing, you looked at your damaged fingernails, the papery skin on your fingers, the veins sketching out trees over your arms, you examined the empty houses lining the street, the dark windows of dark apartments, the stars, the shining moon. You read and reread the plaque on which Alcina Baïadji had set out to inscribe ALCINA BAÏADJI, SHAMANICALLY ASSISTED PROCREATION in Uyghur characters, but had actually written ALCINA BAÏADJI,

SHAMANICALLY ASSISTED COPULATION. Your gaze wandered on, you never thought of pointing out this mistake, this confusion of one word for another. Even then, a new era was dawning, and not only the human species but even the meaning of language was dying away. You felt relaxed, mildly curious about what would come next. You and Alcina Baïadji had held a rehearsal the previous Friday, you knew in detail all the motions she would ask you to make. In any case, Alcina Baïadji would stay in the room all through it. At no point would you be left alone with the man.

You'd said: 'Are you sure he's coming?' And Alcina Baïadji assured you he was, she was perfectly sure of it, that his name was Witold Yanschog, that he bore some resemblance to Enzo Mardirossian, that the resemblance was naturally very slight, but that there was something there all the same, that his silhouette recalled Enzo Mardirossian's when Enzo emerged from the camps. And you asked: 'But what about this man, was he in the camps as well?' And Alcina Baïadji swore that he had been, that he'd spent nineteen years behind the barbed wire, and that, in keeping with your request, he would refrain from speaking, so that you might more easily imagine it was Enzo Mardirossian inside you, and no one else.

The moon sailed on over your heads, casting a bright glow over the walls. Geckos were crawling around Alcina Baïadji's drum.

You knew there was no more than one chance in fifty-eight billion that something might come of your procreative act, if indeed the encounter went that far. The number didn't much matter; more than anything, it signified that humanity was lost. Reflecting that at some point you would have to remove your underwear and let the man rummage inside you with his member, you felt a flood of shame come over you, but you comforted yourself with the thought that Enzo Mardirossian would have urged you to embrace the principle of this session, in the name of the survival of the species. In the name of that minuscule possibility of a pathetic survival of the species. 'Are you sure he's not a partisan of capitalism?' you went on. 'Bella, I promise he's not a nouveau riche,' Alcina Baïadji answered. 'He works for a rubble-removal company. He's a rubble-clearer.'

Little pools of moonlight were scattered all over the sand. A breeze whispered over the top of the dune, beside you. The air was still stifling hot. You wiped a bit of sweat from your neck, from around your mouth, from your eyes. Three dogs emerged from the darkness and crossed the western end of the street, never growling or barking. 'You understand, I wouldn't like to be penetrated by an admirer of the capitalist system,' you said. Alcina Baïadji did her best to reassure you, first with her words and then with a sip of alcohol, and then the rhythm of your conversation waned. Soon, sleep began to visit you in little two- or three-second bursts. It was becoming clear that the man would not appear that night.

Now Alcina Baïadji pensively fingered her magic instruments, dusted them off, picked them up, lay them down again. With the back of her hand she swept away the ants streaming toward the vial of lubricant. Mistakenly, she'd assumed that the session would take place in the first hour of darkness, and she'd prepared herself accordingly, shedding her clothes so that Witold Yanschog might watch her dance, and dream of her and her naked body as he lay on top of you.

I say you, I use the second person singular to avoid continually saying Bella Mardirossian, and so it won't seem that I only talk about myself and my own experiences.

That was how the solstice night went by.

38

Naïsso Baldakchan

The old women crawled through the crackling grass, circling the yurt.

One of them fell into a coughing fit, probably Solange Bud. Her bronchial tubes had been fraying for the past few weeks, ever since she'd dreamt she was inhaling chlorine. In her dream, she was sitting with several wolves by a contaminated pond, smoke rising from the water. As best they could determine in the darkness, the entire landscape was green, a very deep green. The lake, on the other hand, had a yellow-black tint. Absolutely nothing shone in the sky. Haunting music could be heard in the background, a quartet playing Naïsso Baldakchan's *Third Golde Song*. The wolves choked back the desire to howl that often gripped them on such occasions, provoked by the music or the ambience. Some of them lay with their heads between their front paws, moving only their eyes, questioningly. Others had curled up into a ball. These ones were dead.

The *Third Golde Song* had never been performed since its composition, two hundred eighty-one years before. Naïsso Baldakchan still wandered through the dreams of a few scattered souls, often women, very elderly women, but no one bothered to decipher his scores, forever decreed too subtly or brutally distant from what the human ear expects, assuming that the human ear expects something. For nearly two centuries, no sheaf of papers signed Naïsso Baldakchan had been placed on any music stand anywhere.

Also, all the violinists, violists, and cellists had been wiped from the face of the earth. Nowadays, if you wanted to hear the *Seven Golde Songs*, your only hope was to wait for a propitious slumber to come over you. Then you could realize that the ostracism inflicted on Baldakchan was without foundation. There was no brutality in Baldakchan's harmonies, nothing grimly intellectual about his melodies. They were terribly moving. It is true that the audience now judging Baldakchan's work was far closer to the ideal listeners he had in mind as he composed: living wolves, immortal pluricentenarians, dead wolves.

Will Scheidmann lay half slumped over Varvalia Lodenko's bed. The yurt had deteriorated considerably since Varvalia Lodenko set off to rectify her grandson's misdeeds. Will Scheidmann never did feel at home there, and he'd touched nothing in the sixteen years since he was pardoned and offered these lodgings. He always stayed behind when the old women went off nomadizing, and so had never dismantled the tent. Eventually the crosspieces that held up the cloth ceiling had rotted away, leading to the structure's partial collapse. Will Scheidmann stood up and slowly advanced toward the felt rectangle over the door. He walked like an invalid. The leathery algae erupting all over his body hobbled his gait, caught between his legs, rustled.

'Scheidmann!' someone shouted.

'Scheidmann, we're here, what are you doing in there?' another old woman chided.

'I'm coming!' he shouted.

Again those same demanding voices, always the same, piercing his memory back to its most primitive layers, back to the stratum of his birth and even before, back to the time of the dormitory, where his grandmothers manipulated his embryonic form and growled over his body to fill him with their vision of the world.

He pushed the curtain aside and went out. For five minutes he stood on the threshold, solid as a yak.

'I was listening to a quartet by Baldakchan,' he said.

They came nearer. They'd fallen into the disagreeable habit of clutching at the strips of skin that had turned him into a repugnant bush of flesh. Sometimes they pulled hard enough to tear one off. In spite of their entreaties, he still refused to give them more than one strange narract per day, and they tried to compensate with these strips. Once they'd managed to get hold of a kelp-like ribbon of flesh, they went off and examined it at great length, sniffing at it, taking little bites from it, convinced that this might restore the snippets of memory lost in the abyss of time and senility. They fully understood the difference between an ignoble kelp-strip and a strange narract, but this was the way they had found to soothe their withdrawal. Sometimes Will Scheidmann let them to do as they pleased, sometimes not.

'Don't come any closer,' he ordered. 'We were listening to the *Third Golde Song*. Solange Bud was there. We were all on the bank of the pond, sitting in the dark and admiring the yellow moire effect. The chlorine was evaporating in long dancing swirls. Next to me a wolf had just died. His name was Battal Mevlido.'

'A brown wolf with a thick gray tail and a beige spot on his muzzle? Lame from a bullet wound in the rear right paw?' asked Solange Bud.

Will Scheidmann grumbled. He didn't like to be interrupted when he was reciting a strange narract.

'No,' he said. 'He looked red to me in the greenish glow of the chlorine. He didn't limp.'

'Well, it wasn't Battal Mevlido, then,' murmured Solange Bud, and she began to cough again.

All around him, the old women were reaching out to pull off a piece of his flesh. Solange Bud coughed and coughed, horribly. Scheidmann took a step back.

'I called him Battal Mevlido, but it was me,' he said. 'I gave him that name so I wouldn't seem to be forever speaking of myself, and never of anyone else. But it was me.'

39

Linda Siew

One night, when the traffic was sparse on the Avenue Meyerberh, Abacheïev saw a lamp come on in the big apartment block on the Boulevard des Rambutans. Then it went off again. Several times over the following evenings, he noted the presence of that light. Someone had settled in on the fifth floor. Statistically, the chances were good that it was a woman, or at least one chance in two. Solitude was weighing heavy on Abacheïev's shoulders, and he decided to prepare a meal for his new neighbor, and bring it to her door.

Abacheïev knew the recipes for several elaborate dishes, but at the moment he lacked the ingredients. He spent three days gathering everything he would need for his menu: a Mongol sauté of lamb on the one hand, and on the other a green chicken curry.

Then he set to work.

He began with the lamb. For want of more appropriate meats, he was forced to replace the lamb and chicken with seagulls, whose cadavers he'd found on the banks of the Kanal. Their bodies were heavy and imposing. He plucked and boned them beside the Kanal's murky waters.

Stripping away the remaining skin, he cut the flesh into slices for the sauté and larger chunks for the curry, dropping the slices into a marinade of ginger, garlic, soy sauce, sesame oil, and rice wine. He scattered a spoonful of cornstarch over the top and stirred.

An odor of animal flesh clung to his hands, more disagreeable than the garlic and ginger. Briskly he soaped his palms. The gulls he'd butchered were of an uncertain species; they weren't laughing gulls, and in any case they were dead. The most pungent aroma came from the folds under their wings, but the rest of their bodies smelled strongly too. Abacheïev washed his hands again. He couldn't stand that filthy bird stench on his person.

Next he had to break open a coconut and collect the milk. Abacheïev grated the meat and squeezed it until he'd filled two bowls with liquid. He added some hot green chilies from which he'd removed the seeds; in another pan, he fried several shreds of red chili, three pinches of coriander seeds, some shrimp paste, and some cumin.

The scent of the smoking spices drifted around him. Abacheïev transferred them to a mortar and pounded them for some time with the remaining ginger and garlic, then fried the resulting paste in oil and added it to the spiced coconut milk, in which the pieces of the biggest gull were already simmering, along with the wings of the smallest.

The golden rule, when you're making several dishes at once, is to coordinate the crucial cooking stages with great care, so as not to sacrifice one dish for another. You have to keep control of the passing moments. Last-minute peeling, for instance, can have disastrous consequences. Abacheïev was well aware of this, and he'd taken care to do all the mincing and chopping beforehand. Taking advantage of a lull in his anxious surveillance of the pans, he cut an onion into thin crescents and filled a cup with the contents of a small bag of sesame seeds, to be scattered over the sauté of lamb just before serving. Then he went to get the lime he would squeeze over the curry in the last few moments of its simmering, and he placed it within easy reach.

Now he did some washing, and the disorder receded. He dried off the mortar and the other utensils, and put them away.

The kitchen was filled with aromas. The rather disturbingly dominant emanations of the shrimp paste had finally harmonized with the sweeter perfumes that surrounded it. The curry was nearing completion. Abacheïev added three spoonfuls of peanut butter and lowered the flame. There would be no rice to accompany this meal. Knowing that he could not carry more than two dishes at once, Abacheïev had made that decision. From a dietetic point of view this was unfortunate, but, objectively, it was unavoidable.

Abacheïev added fresh oil to the frying pan. The oil sputtered, and he tossed in the onion, which he would brown slightly before searing the lamb or its ersatz.

Just then the gas went off.

Very quickly, the oil's gentle hiss died away.

Abacheïev groaned. Gas outages could go on for days. By thermic inertia, the curry continued to bubble feebly before him.

Abacheïev pulled the lever to shut off the gas. He groaned again, but he still hadn't lost control of the situation. He would simply modify his menu, and offer his neighbor a tartare of gull along with the chicken curry. There was every reason to hope that the marinade had flavored and tenderized the raw meat. He sprinkled the curry with lime juice, scattered the tartare with the sesame seeds and the lukewarm crescents of onion. The two dishes were a pleasure to behold.

Now Abacheïev could leave his apartment.

He had some difficulty crossing the avenue. The automobiles were numerous, and the dishes balanced in his arms forbade zigzags or great leaps forward. Nevertheless, he soon found himself on the other side. He headed toward the Boulevard des Rambutans.

Evening had begun to fall. The streetlights lit an empty sidewalk, without a pedestrian in sight. The women piloting their vehicles slowed to a crawl as they pulled alongside Abacheïev, but their names could be read for only a fraction of a second, as they quickly turned off the lights over their plates.

One of them was named Yashreene Kogan.

Another drove past, identified by her plate as Linda Siew.

The curry was going cold, and Abacheïev picked up his pace.

After this his trail vanishes. Did Abacheïev succeed in trans-porting his neighborly offerings undisturbed? Was he welcomed warmly or with hostility? Did he manage to reach the fifth floor? Might he not have been accosted well before, as soon as he turned the corner of the Boulevard des Rambutans, by Yashreene Kogan or Linda Siew? Was his hot dish appreciated or spurned? And his cold dish? Among the foods on offer that night, which one was eaten first?

40

Dick Jerichoe

Now, listen carefully. I'm not joking anymore. What matters is not whether the things I'm telling you are realistic or not, skillfully recounted or not, surrealistic or not, inscribed or not within the postexotic tradition, or if I spin out these sentences in a murmur of fear or a howl of indignation, or with infinite tenderness for everything that moves, or if, behind my voice, behind what it is customary to call my voice, one can or cannot make out a heartfelt appeal for radical combat against the real or merely a schizophrenic helplessness in the face of the real, or an attempt at an egalitarian epic, darkened or not by despair and disgust at the present or future. That is not the question. Nor even whether Will Scheidmann lived before or after such unknown but essential novelists as Lutz Bassmann or Fred Zenfl or Artem Veselyi, in the days of the camps and the prisons, or, say, shortly after, or two centuries or nine centuries after, or if the language of the men and women speaking here or silent here is related to the Altaic dialects, or dominated by Chinese or Slavic influences, or is, on the contrary, closer to the shamanic tongues of the Rockies or Andes, or something more arcane yet. That is absolutely not the question. The material I offer here is in no way meant to give rise to such speculations. I propose no ideology of poetic distortion or of magical or metaphorical transmutation of the world. I speak the language of today and none other. Everything I tell you here is one hundred percent true, whether I say it partially, or allusively, or pretentiously, or barbarically, or whether I turn circles around it without really saying it. Everything happened exactly as I describe it, everything has already taken place just like this at some moment of your life or mine, or will take place later, in reality or in our dreams. In that sense, it's all very simple. The images speak for themselves, without artifice; they contain nothing other than themselves and those speaking. That's why there's no place here for numerical tallies or objective accounts.

Take for example the corrective epic of Varvalia Lodenko, her appeals for a massacre of the powerful, her nostalgia for a total abolition of every sort of privilege. The question is not whether this is only a right-minded daydream, or if Varvalia Lodenko's rifle did indeed resound in the real, or if it is preparing to do so. That is absolutely not the question. Here and there I have told you of Varvalia Lodenko's travels from town to town, preaching a return to maximalism and unhesitatingly enacting her own minimalist struggle, founded first and foremost on the physical elimination of those newly reappeared from nothingness, the exploiters and the mafiosi and the apologists of exploitation and of the mafia, and then secondarily on the dismantling of all the mechanisms of economic inequality and an immediate halt to all circulation of dollars. It has been said that this woman left a long trail of capitalist blood behind her, which is another way of saying that, in her wake, no difference remained between rich and poor, between the privileged and the penniless. Thus, after Varvalia Lodenko had passed by, people were finally at ease to live their little lives fraternally once again, to build new ruins without shame, or, at least, to live without shame in the endless ruins before them. These facts have nothing to do with novelistic invention; they coincide with a truth that is one hundred percent true, and they do not deserve to be weighed down by superfluous lyrical flourishes.

There is one aspect of this story that has not yet been mentioned, however, and that is perhaps the only detail to which I will return here. Varvalia Lodenko was not always alone in her labors. Whenever we were informed of her impending arrival in one town or another, we arranged to have her welcomed with a brass band, a banner, and some pemmican, along with some milk alcohol when we could get hold of it. By we, I mean here a handful of inhabitants of the Kanal neighborhood, such as myself and Dick Jerichoe and Dick's companion Careen Jerichoe. I played the harmonica, Careen sang, Dick Jerichoe backed us up on the alto rebec. He was nothing much as an altoist, but his pemmican was unsurpassed. Fearing that Varvalia Lodenko might not enjoy a welcome as friendly as ours in her travels to come, we'd assumed the role of an itinerant orchestra, and we went on ahead of her in all her transcontinental wanderings. We always brought a supply of cudgels along with our instruments. Often we had to walk through devastation for years at a time to get from one city to the next. As in the time of humanity's beginnings, the distances were not on the human scale. A few clusters of population remained on the planet, near Lake Hövsgöl, or the banks of the Mekong or the Orbise, and in a few last little towns that had served as the capital, one after the other, depending on actuarial and climatic trends, and whose names have all faded from my memory, with the notable exception of Luang Prabang. One of Varvalia Lodenko's favorite musicians was Kaanto Djylas. I always included a madrigal by Djylas in our program. She listened, smoking her acrid pipe, then went off into the depths of the ruins to sleep; the next day, after a look around the place, she set off once again on her mission to rip out the human roots of unhappiness. Sometimes I gave her a hand assassinating someone or other. Will Scheidmann's wicked decrees hadn't hastened the disappearance of the human species, but they hadn't slowed it either. The birthrate was now next to nothing. In order for a fertilization to lead somewhere, it had to be done our way, among us old folks. Deep in the ruins, I sometimes gave Varvalia Lodenko a hand with that, too.

41

Costanzo Cossu

The last ferry was casting off. Khrili Gompo heard the mooring ropes fall into the mud; he heard the cranks creaking, and then the paddle-blades clapping against the still waters, and also, from the other side of the dock, from the palm-wood lattice hut where the ticket-seller spent his nights on the wrong side of the river, he heard a plaintive voice. 'It doesn't matter,' the voice was saying, 'I was really thinking of crossing tomorrow anyway.' And then the voice went on, persistent, 'I'll go tomorrow morning. The first ferry's cheaper, right? . . .'

Khrili Gompo sat facing the river. The light glinted off the oily ripples of the water's surface, and cast a reddish gold glow over the dense fronds of the trees on the opposite bank, eight hundred meters away. Beyond that nothing much could be seen, only an endless rolling expanse of green, for the forest continued, uninhabited and immense, after the river and the narrow band of stilted houses and temples.

The sun was setting.

Gompo squinted, his back against a coconut tree. He had sixteen minutes to go. 'I don't care about the schedule,' the voice was now saying. 'What I'm really interested in is the discount that . . .'

'Discount?' the ferry worker finally replied. 'On what grounds?'

Khrili Gompo leaned against the rotting scales of the coconut tree, feigning sleep. He'd chosen an unfortunate spot. As often happens at dusk, hundreds of winged ants were dropping from the leaves where they'd spent the day, letting themselves fall to the ground. Gompo sat directly in their path, and a rain of insects fell over him, blackening his shoulders and arms, and the top of his head. He made no move to brush them away, for fear of attracting attention.

'Well,' said the man, 'how about as a refugee? . . .'

'That won't get you a discount,' the other one said.

'Oh,' said the first man, disappointed, and then he began to enumerate all the physical and mental failings afflicting him, and all the sorrows that had assailed him, him and his loved ones, in the past and more recently. None of this earned him the right to a half-price fare. 'My name is Costanzo Cossu,' he finally said. 'It's a clown's name. In some places entertainers cross for free. Not here?'

The ferry was soundlessly gliding away. There was no one left on this side of the river but Gompo, the ticket seller, and Costanzo Cossu. Lost in their oratorical joust, the two men never glanced at the ragged figure sitting some ten meters away, his back to a tree, seemingly asleep. Their own appearance was scarcely impressive: torn shirts and caps, filthy shorts, unstitched sandals summarily repaired with strands of raffia. The ferry worker had a rucksack over his shoulder; Costanzo Cossu's only luggage was a plastic bag adorned with the address of a supermarket. Together they would soon have compiled an exhaustive list of all the states of distress offering no advantage to travelers. Costanzo Cossu suggested rationales for exemptions or rebates, and the watchman refused them. 'What if they took me on board as accompanied baggage?' offered Costanzo Cossu. 'Or in the Untermensch category? I'll curl up among the packages, I'll stay perfectly still, I won't complain if they throw filthy bundles on top of me. No?'

'No.'

There was something timeless in the evening calm. Following the riverbank, a white heron disappeared downstream. Beyond the banana groves, the red glow of the sky was dimming. A bluish mist was already veiling the curve of the river. The cicadas stopped shrieking, a buffalo bellowed, the road to the landing stage was aswarm with mosquitos, a toad croaked, on the opposite bank tiny fishermen were lifting a small square net into a tiny boat, lights flickered on here and there, the ferry was now only a distant spot on the ocher waters. Something made an aqualung sound inside Khrili Gompo's skull, alerting him that another minute had passed. Dozens of winged ants were swarming over his neck. 'Suppose you put me down as a cadaver? . . . As miscellaneous merchandise?' the man suggested. 'As a found object?'

Droplets of sweat beaded under Gompo's nose, behind his ears, on his neck, then trickled earthward. 'Sometimes I have nightmares where I see a woman named Barbe,' Costanzo Cossu was saying. 'That's worth something off, isn't it? . . . Even a little?'

'Or suppose I was an extraterrestrial?' he suddenly blurted out.

Then came a whispered sentence, and the two men drew nearer together. Khrili Gompo saw their insistent gaze streaming toward him. Costanzo Cossu had a wild look about him. 'An extraterrestrial covered with ants?' he threw out, contemptuously.

Gompo shivered. This was the second time in three hundred years that he'd been openly denounced as a stranger to the terrestrial realm. And, baseless or not, he found this suspicion terrifically unpleasant.

42

Patricia Yashree

After thirty-two years of sordid, dead calm, I had a dream in which people assured me they'd seen Sophie Gironde. For three decades I'd been pining after her, and if I wanted to go on believing I might see her again, I would have to embed myself in that dream and await her.

It was one of those dreams where nothing really frightening happens, but every minute is suffused with a strong sense of disquiet. Dusk hung over the city at all hours, and it was easy to lose your way. Some neighborhoods had disappeared under the sand, others not. Whenever I looked into the street, I saw birds dying. They broke out of their glide, bounced mutely off the asphalt with a pathetic thump; then, after a moment, they stopped writhing.

I settled into that dream, and into that city. There were millions of abandoned buildings, their doors torn off for fuel, like everywhere else, which meant that you had to look in the most out of the way places to find decent housing. I took over a three-room apartment on the edge of the red dunes. Existence went on, neither dangerous nor pleasant. I was entrusted with a number of vague occupations, tasks of no particular nature; in the end, they offered me steady work near the incinerators. I say they to suggest that some social structure was then in place, but the fact is I was alone.

Ten months later, I saw Sophie Gironde.

She was walking down the Avenue des Archers with a man and

woman I'd met in the camps, three hundred twenty-seven years before: Patricia Yashree and Tchinguiz Black.

I called after them. Together they turned around, and at all once they began to wave and gesticulate.

We embraced. Sophie Gironde had put on weight. She seemed sad. For a few minutes she brazenly rubbed her body against mine, as if we were the only two left in the world. She exhaled her intoxicating shaman temptress breath into my face, touching my hips and shoulder blades, and we stood there like that, suspended in the uncertain light, unable to speak the slightest syllable, unable even to form one nostalgic or constructive thought, conscious only of our lack of passion and of the seconds speeding by around us, and of the crows pelting the asphalt, knocked senseless, and the black vultures, hornbills, mynahs, and pigeons.

After a moment, Patricia Yashree came to our side. She draped us in a black shawl she'd been wearing over her shoulders, and then she embraced us both. With unbelieving tenderness, the three of us swayed back and forth on the sidewalk, exchanging confused carnal messages, sorry not to be more greatly moved than we were, for, truth be told, we were failing to fully relish the moment.

Waiting for this intimate scene to run its course, Tchinguiz Black had squatted down by the gutter, in the position assumed by the Mongols in the Batomga camp during their breaks. He lit a pipe and gazed over the street through the smoke. A magnetic storm was coming. The air was full of mauve depths, now and then shot through with slow, snaking bolts of lightning, hairy, sluggish sparks, marble-like veins of ozone.

Later, as we walked toward the neighborhood of the great dunes, Sophie Gironde pointed toward the Rue du Lac-Ayane. A little crowd had gathered by a movie theater, of which there remained only the facade. They were standing in line, as if a show were soon to begin.

'Be careful,' said Tchinguiz Black. 'It might be a trap.'

We came nearer, still maintaining a respectful distance from the crowd. There were fourteen people, all of them appallingly dirty, their hair matted and even crusty, their faces even more sinister than mine. They stood waiting in the semidarkness. Their gazes refused to meet ours.

The last showing had taken place at least three centuries before. The poster had spent the intervening years going irretrievably brown in its glass case, but a few letters could still be made out, and with them the title: *Before Schlumm*. It was a full-length film that they'd also shown us at Batomga, a very bad film.

'I want to go in,' Patricia Yashree suddenly said.

'No, please,' begged Tchinguiz Black, but she was already out of earshot.

She slipped into the crowd of strange movie-goers. For two or three minutes she remained in view; then a collective movement ran through the crowd, and as they pushed forward she disappeared. After a moment they fell still again, and then I could no longer tell her apart from the rest.

'She won't be back,' said Tchinguiz Black.

'Let's wait a while all the same,' I said.

We sat down on a pile of sand across from the theater. Sophie Gironde sank down alongside me, then sat up. She didn't say a word. She really was much fatter than I remembered her, less sure of herself and, it seemed to me, not so determined to live.

The magnetic wind hissed and crackled five meters over our heads.

Still more birds came crashing to the ground, beside us, in the street, in the sand. To ease his anxiety, Tchinguiz Black went off to identify them, measuring them from beak to tail and wingtip to wingtip with a tape he'd pulled from his pocket. When the numbers were of a truly abnormal nature, he dropped the bird with a brief cry of disgust and looked up; our eyes met, trying to start a dialogue that refused to take.

With Tchinguiz Black I shared our years in the camp, an unproductive interest in ornithology, a sinister physiognomy, and also these two women, Sophie Gironde and Patricia Yashree, and the fear of having lost one of them forever, and a negative opinion of the film *Before Schlumm*; but we no longer knew how to speak together, or how to be silent together.

43

Maria Clementi

As on every sixteenth of October for what will soon be one thousand one hundred and eleven years, I dreamt last night that I was named Will Scheidmann, even though my name is Clementi, Maria Clementi.

I awoke with a start. I saw the moon trembling through the grill over the window, round and small, colored a sordid ivory. It had a fever, and couldn't stop its strange shivering. Also, I have an illness that affects my night vision. Spots of light drift or dart through the images before me whenever I open my eyes. No sound of human origin lurked in the building around me. My breath had no companion. There's a cracked pipe at the end of the hall, and below it a bucket someone put there one day. The dripping water resounded down the hallway, like echoing drops in a deep well. The night air streamed in under my door. Everything stank around me. I wanted to go back to sleep. On the pillow lay a handful of gray hairs, lost as I slept. My breath stank like a filthy dog's.

After a minute my dream started up again, and once again I'd been cast as Will Scheidmann. I use the passive voice with some regret, of course, not knowing the name of my dream's director.

I'd known Scheidmann for many years, but he'd deteriorated in a way I would have found hard to imagine if this dream hadn't allowed me into his flesh. His volume had changed. His body had sprouted, and no longer conformed to the norms of the animal realm. Immense matted scales, some brittle, some not, grew from what must once have been the top of his skull, or his shoulders or waist, or the stove that once spewed smoke into Varvalia Lodenko's yurt.

I could feel the empty steppe beneath me, riddled with absence, without insects or livestock or forage, a dead land, long since communicating with nothing. Everyone had disappeared but the old women, or what remained of them, which is to say very little, actually. The days passed by without end, interspersed with odiously empty nights. Rains of shooting stars were erupting several times a week now, accentuating the redness of the soil and even its Martian quality. The meteorites gave off disagreeable gases. Often you couldn't breathe for hours at a time.

Broken down and amnesic, too frail now to seize my skins with their fingers or mouths and ruminate the sap, the old women crawled in circles through the surrounding terrain. Devoid of emotion or nostalgia, they orbited slowly around me, immortal, ill-equipped to go on living but not knowing how to die, sometimes drumming on a fragment of kettle or hammering at the iron framework that once bolstered their skeletons, sometimes beseeching me with vague gesticulations to invent more strange narracts, again and again, no matter the circumstances. Despite his metamorphosis and notwithstanding the advance of the nothingness around him, Will Scheidmann had indeed continued to tell a story every day, perhaps because he had nothing else to say or do, or because his compassion for his grandmothers was madly obedient, or for some other reason that no one would ever bring to light. Since his audience no longer reacted to his stories, and since everything was now defunct, to the horizon and beyond, he didn't always articulate his anecdotes through to the end, and sometimes he only whispered an outline of their events, but, no matter what, through thick and thin, he came up with something new every day. He set out his narracts in bunches of forty-nine. To each stack he gave a number or title.

That night, that October 16, I suggested he give his next bunch the name *Minor Angels*. I'd once used this title for a romånce, in other circumstances and in another world, but I thought it well suited to the summum that Scheidmann was now finishing, the last bunch of all.

The moon was blurred by my dream and a rain of shooting stars. A thousand times over, the incandescent stones punched through the night and pierced the ground with a high-pitched shriek, a tiny cosmic twittering.

Sometimes they hit me, and I awoke. I heard the star rebounding at my feet, hissing a moment longer, and then falling silent. My eyes couldn't adjust to the darkness. I gazed at the trembling moon, through the grill, on the other side of the wall. From time to time the light flickered out completely. I no longer knew if I was Will Scheidmann or Maria Clementi, I said I purely at random, I didn't know who was speaking inside me or what minds had conceived me or were observing me. I didn't know if I was a dead man or a dead woman or if I was going to die. I thought of the animals that perished before me and of the humans now disappeared and I wondered whom I might stand before one day to recite *Minor Angels*. To add to my confusion, I wasn't sure what might lie behind that title: a strange romånce or simply a bundle of forty-nine strange narracts.

And suddenly I was just like the old women, numb before the interminable. I didn't know how to die, and, rather than speak, I moved my fingers in the darkness. I could hear nothing more. And I listened.

44

Rim Scheidmann

Varvalia Lodenko smashed the lock with her rifle and entered the room. Chickens cackled, flapping their wings in a shower of dirt and feathers and utensils and plastic bottles. A shelf had collapsed in the uproar, in the excitement, in the lunar half-light, dumping its contents not far from the bed where capitalism's last mafioso lay outstretched. The room stank of poultry and gangrene. The last mafioso reached out and switched on the bedside lamp. His face was ashen. An expression of anxious fatalism gradually reappeared on his features, his lips twisted to form a nonexistent word. Faced with this threat, he threw off the blanket and rolled onto his side. Eight days before, Varvalia Lodenko had wounded him above the knee, leaving a trail of blood that led her back to this den. A filthy bandage mummified his thigh. After a half-minute, the last mafioso's niece entered in turn. She was not a capitalist. She worked for the census, with veterinarians and statisticians; she knew that the human population now consisted of thirty-five individuals, including herself, Will Scheidmann, the immortals, and the last representative of the capitalist underworld, this latter soon to be dead. She shrugged her shoulders. She was pregnant; in her ventral pouch she bore a child she'd made almost single-handed, with the help of a veterinarian. It was a girl, already christened Rim Scheidmann, who would bring order, camps, and fraternity back to the world. She went and leaned on the windowsill without so much as a glance toward her uncle. Outside, she could see the surroundings of the Avenue du Kanal, the brick-colored dunes, the moon exhausted from its battle with the clouds. With a knife, Varvalia cut a slit below the mafioso's thoracic cage and thrust in her hand, as the Mongols do, feeling her way until her fingers found his aorta. She gave it a pinch, squeezing the heart in her palm. This was a seventeenth of October. In her thoughts, the niece of the last rich man went on wandering with her child through what remained of the universe.

Now Varvalia Lodenko was trying to break the table lamp. Several times she threw it to the floor, but the object only rolled away, unbroken. She picked it up with her blood-drenched hand and turned off the light.

45

Dora Fennimore

Shoved and jostled day and night, Dora Fennimore had lost all sense of balance. She had to huddle against Schlomo Bronx for all she was worth, exerting a terrible pressure on his left lung, hip, and leg. After a few days, Schlomo Bronx realized that his skin had ceased to constitute a barrier, that their two bodies had torn open and melded into one. By my calculations, this came at the dawn of October 18. I loved Dora Fennimore, I loved her enough not to mind her melding into me, leaving me heavier and more pain-filled and odd in my musculature. Suddenly I realized she was afraid. My arms were clamped between still other bodies, and I had no way to free them and reassure her with a caress. My weariness and my position prevented me from turning toward her and smiling. I regret this, because I believe she would have been happy to see my smile directed her way. I'd spent this first week of the transfer whispering all the affectionate words we'd invented in the course of our life together, knowing the day would come when we'd find ourselves shoved in with strangers, exchanging our love as if we were alone, as if nothing were happening around us. I don't know if she could hear me. She had no strength to answer. From the first moments of the journey, I heard her gasping for breath among the panting carcasses and their nauseating darkness. When I say I, I refer in part to Schlomo Bronx, but only in part; I am also thinking of Ionathan Leefschetz and Izmaïl Dawkes, crammed so close against me that our collarbones had split open and mingled, and of others as well, beyond Leefschetz, now incorporated into our collective flesh. Among these latter I will mention Fred Zenfl, for whom this trip was not a first, who stood jammed into a corner, his nape squeezed and twisted, his head pinned to the walls by a woman who had the misfortune of being pregnant, and who lay upright, sobbing, without a gesture, without a word, her weight crushing the men and women around her. There was a gap between the planks before my eyes, and sometimes, in little bursts, when the daylight outside could be distinguished from darkness, I could see what was happening there, or, when nothing was happening, I could take in the setting in which something might happen. Standing across from me, on the starboard side, Fred Zenfl must have enjoyed the same privilege, the same visual possibilities, for he later told of what he had seen in a little book called The Seven Last Lieder, composed of seven rather disappointing murmuracts, unquestionably one of his worst texts. But what he says there bears little resemblance to what I saw from the port side, which I related aloud, in hopes of entertaining my comrades and myself. It was a landscape of autumnal forests that Fred Zenfl saw speeding past through the planks, the sort of landscape that nearly always so splendidly presages the camps, and he saw piles of felled larches and dark little lakes and guard posts and rusted vats, rusting trucks, hangars, crumbling barracks, sometimes herds of reindeer hidden among the trees, sometimes smoke, and sometimes hundreds of kilometers without a living soul to be seen. But it was a different sort of spectacle I saw through the cracks before me, and almost inevitably an urban landscape. Deserted avenues followed empty crossroads and abandoned roadways; apart from the wolves and a few begging shadows, the ruins were sparsely inhabited. Sometimes, in an elevator shaft or at an intersection, the cannibals could be seen laying into one of their victims, but in general there was nothing that might serve as material for an anecdote, and I preferred to look into myself, into my recent memories, for the elements of my account. I said, for instance: 'Last night, I dreamt once again that I was walking with Dora Fennimore on the Rue du Kanal.' And, after one or two seconds of silence, I added: 'Dora Fennimore was wearing a stunning dress.' And, when asked for further vestimentary details, I said, 'A long Chinese dress, with a slit, deep blue, and shocking pink lapels.' I waited for the sighs of wonderment to die down, and then I said, 'The ambience of the Rue du Kanal was precisely that of the scenes I now see through the planks.' And, having no choice but to continue, since they urged me to press forward, I said, 'Which is to say that it wasn't clear whether the atmosphere was enchanting or extremely sinister.' Then: 'For example, the air was full of soaring birds and huge butterflies, better adapted than we to the new social and climatic conditions.' And, when a voice behind me asked just what these creatures looked like, I said: 'Winged, of an extraordinary gray, cut from velvety organic materials, with rich black eyes watching the inside of our dreams.' And, after a pause, I added, 'Dora Fennimore and I walked under their wings, our only thought to go on living.' And, a little later, I completed this idea, saying: 'We were together in the twilight, we listened to the sounds of the wings in the sky, we breathed one against the other as we listened, knowing there was nothing to say, and from time to time we lay down on the sidewalk to embrace more completely, or approached the palisades and squinted to peer through the planks, and from time to time a bird fell nearby, taking off the corner of an apartment building as it passed, or reducing the building to rubble, in perfect silence, without a single cry from inside.'

46

Sengül Mizrakiev

The murmur of falling water suddenly swelled to a roar, then faltered and faded away. It was raining on the edge of the blackness. Since the time had not yet begun to elapse, the shower came to a hesitant end. After a few last isolated drops, silence reigned once more.

Khrili Gompo coughed, not because of the damp, but because he hadn't breathed for a week, and his orifices were clogged with soot from the crossing. The force of his cough unplugged various tiny conduits within him, and behind his inner ear he heard a voice reminding him of his name, Gompo, and of his mission, to collect a store of images that might help us to better understand the world. He'd drifted far from the initial objective, but at least he'd finally stabilized somewhere. The calendar showed the date as October 19, a Monday. It was my voice speaking in his ear. I informed him that this would be his final dive, and that it would last approximately eleven minutes and nine seconds.

Khrili Gompo found himself standing near a bakery. Overcome by a wrenching nausea, he approached the display window and slowly let himself slide to the ground. He squatted on the sidewalk in the posture of an Aztec mummy, the preferred pose for our activities, knees touching his shoulders, arms around his knees, his torso somewhat slack, as after a final sigh. To his right hovered an aroma of praline. To his left, a basement smell wafted from a little low window. The shop was closed.

For four minutes, Gompo's only activity was a struggle against the desire to vomit. A stream of pedestrians passed by, some in raincoats, some Paleozoic in their physiognomy, others accompanied by dogs or even cats that noticed Gompo's presence and strained at their leashes to go sniff at him. An old woman in a false alpaca jacket bent down to drop a coin between his feet, say a half-dollar. Events were accelerating, but the harvest of information remained meager. Hoping to broaden his view of the universe, Khrili Gompo rose to his feet, automatically assuming the beggar position.

A street sign told him he was on the Rue des Ardoises. There was nothing of architectural note to be seen. The street was narrow and sloped.

A certain Sengül Mizrakiev approached, and placed a coin into his outstretched hand, say a dollar. After a moment's hesitation, he asked him the time. Khrili Gompo did not think to raise his left wrist to his eyes; rather, he painstakingly translated the reading I was then offering him, which was that he had five minutes and forty-nine seconds to go.

'It's about five minutes and forty-seven seconds before the end,' said Khrili Gompo.

'Oh,' said the man.

He stood before Gompo, uncertain, beginning to notice the loathsome carboniferous effluvia streaming from Gompo's tattered clothes. Suddenly he went pale.

'Oh, who cares, anyway,' he said.

Khrili Gompo agreed. The man wore a navy-blue sweater with a misshapen collar, and he had an intelligent air, the look of someone who knew how to read, who might even have read one or two of Fred Zenfl's novels. He walked off. No domesticated animal trailed behind him.

After this, and up to the close of the final second, nothing significant happened. It was hardly worth reaspirating Gompo after such mediocre results, so we left him on the Rue des Ardoises.

47

Gloria Tatko

We entered the evacuation passage on October 20, each of us lurching in our own way, each of us clumsily struggling to keep clear of the doors with flames or blood behind them. There were only two of us left. The moon went down, three hours passed by, then the moon appeared again, then the dawn came, then once again the day drew to a close. Gloria Tatko walked on before me. She kept her head down, looking up from below, shaking her hair, like greasy braids, and her arms, like long bundles of vesicular ribbons. It made me sad to see her this way. Soon she would be a horrible thing to behold, like Will Scheidmann as he often appears in the last chapters of Fred Zenfl's books. My vision was clouded by tears. Gloria Tatko turned around. She was five or six meters ahead of me, but it cost her some considerable effort to convey a few unintelligible words through the roar of the fire. 'Hurry up!' she cried in a repulsively oily voice. 'You're going to have to pick up the pace if you want to get to the womb in time! . . . The bears are about to give birth! They're already writhing in pain! . . .' I waved my hand to show Gloria I'd understood her warning. She shouted the first words of another sentence, but, since we were entering an area of turbulence, she did not continue. Rather than hasten my gait, I began to doze as a defensive measure. The buildings were burning around us. Elevators were falling, whistling as they fell, preceded and followed by flaming bodies. There was little light, apart from those scarlet torches and the halo they brought with them in their descent. The moon was nearing its last quarter; two nights later, it no longer lit our way. My face was furrowed by tears, like a mask slowly melting. I followed close behind Gloria Tatko. She'd lost her clothes and hair in the heat. She mumbled admonitions that I could no longer decipher. Not far away, the bears roared in drooling tones. They were suffering terribly, their entrails on fire. The first contractions had begun. The moon reappeared in the form of a slender sickle. Obstinately we continued down the passageway. Certain doors had already been consumed by the flames, others gaped open in their dilapidation. Still others seemed eternal. On one I spotted a number, 885, too familiar not to be sinister. That was the number of my room. We'd gone in a circle. I say my room so as not to lose myself in pointless explanations. Room 885 was where I'd been sequestered since the beginning, in a cell next to the cabin of Sophie Gironde, the woman I love and have never met in reality, because the hallways are laid out in such a way that none of us can ever join with another, real or oneiric, in any relationship that could be called human or real. 'Faster!' Gloria Tatko groaned. 'It's getting late, my boy! . . . It's late already! . . .' I imagined the bears struggling in the gloom below decks, rolling this way and that in their fear and suffering, their fur stained with blood, slamming at the walls with their gigantic paws. The ship was empty, the sailors elsewhere or dead. I could hear Sophie Gironde coming and going from one beast to the next. 'Hurry up, my boy . . .' Gloria Tatko panted. 'See if you can get through on the other side! . . .' She stood lurching amid a spray of flames, showing me the way, the moon hung round above us, there was no way through. I zigzagged my way to cabin 886, to the door's outer side. I pressed my bleeding face to the thick glass of the window. I caught a short glimpse of Sophie Gironde before she disappeared from my field of vision. She was glistening with placenta. The white bears licked their young, growling, gigantic, lying on their backs, in attitudes now playful, now sullen. I pounded the door with my fist. No sound resulted. I heard the bears, and I heard

Sophie Gironde's voice. I don't know what she was saying or who she was talking to. It was too late to go through the doorway and find my way out of this, and into a womb or the open air. 'Ah, my boy . . .' sighed Gloria Tatko. I whirled around to face her, about to return to her side, I couldn't see her, I called out, she made no reply. On that side the sky was dark and starless. Nothing was shining now. A streak of useless afterbirth muddied the only window I might have seen through. Even the flames had stopped glowing now.

48

Alia Araokane

Read Fred Zenfl's books, the ones with no ending as well as the ones he wrote through to the end, the last page always painfully spattered with blood and soot, read the novels he sometimes copied out for his readership in lots of two or even three, some of them might still be found lying in one mass grave or another, ready to read if you brush away the ash that encrusts them and shake out the quicklime that impregnates them and if you don't pay too much mind to your own sobs; others are still half afloat in murky waters, beneath the surface of his dreams or yours, read them even if you've forgotten how to read, love them, often they depict the landscapes of abjection where those who made it through their abjection alive were forced to live and breathe, and you'll also find some marvelous scenes of sensual tenderness, because in spite of everything these novels do not always refuse to speak of amorous fidelity and memory, they're built on what's left when nothing is left, but they depend entirely on you to be admirable, they generally discuss the extinction of everything and everyone, which was Fred Zenfl's brooding preoccupation during and after the camps, read them, seek them out, for many long years Fred Zenfl drifted from camp to camp, so vast was his knowledge of barbed wire that he compiled a dictionary of all its many synonyms in slang, he so loved the concentrationary regions that he longed for the coming of camps for all men and all women, he never stopped writing of misery and the final hallucinations, read for instance *Die sieben letzte Lieder*, one of his very worst texts, or *The 21st of October*, a separate text that is incontestably the worst of all, but which for my part I particularly enjoy, since it says we were companions in our travels and in disaster, and it's true that we wept bitterly together, even though, since most of the time we were far apart, and in saying I here I evoke Alia Araokane, we never actually met, except for one single night, also read my favorite of Fred Zenfl's novels, written as a locomotive was dismembering him and dragging his body down the tracks, a novel so amusing and varied as to please all men and all women, read it, read that one at least, and love it.

49

Verena Yong

Enzo Mardirossian was nowhere to be seen when I finally came to his house. I settled in not far away, eating the provisions I'd been planning to offer him in payment. The weather was turning cold. Sometimes, as daylight was fading, grayish flecks drifted up from the ground, skidding through the air at eye-level, then disappearing. The tear fixer's house had the look of a ruin burned to the ground centuries before, but, having so long been raked by tempests of defoliant and gas, the vegetation had not overwhelmed it. The bushes were stunted, the blackberries ripening among the thorns tasted of niter. Let's say these were the last fruits of the fall, and let's say no more about it. Next I headed toward the well. I climbed down inside and called out. I found only shreds of burned or rotted cloth in the niches where someone might have found shelter. I emerged again on October 22. Outside, the landscape was nearing the end of its transformation into nocturnal mud. I know what the fixer would have told me: that everything within me had gone awry, not only my tears, that I wept any old way, at random, and often for the wrong reason, or for no reason, or else I remained impassive without cause. It was too late for a cure, and finally I decided to forget about the fixer. Already there was almost nothing around me. Guided by a gleam of light, I climbed a small mound of ashes. A woman was lying there, next to a lantern. We struck up an acquaintance, we lived for a moment on the top of the world, we had three children, daughters. One of them took her mother's name, Verena Yong. She was beautiful. Let's say she was the last. After several years, the darkness grew deeper. It was hard to remain where you were, and hard to move without losing your way, and suddenly there was no one answering my calls. Afraid to leave the lantern's halo of light in the darkness, I began to live my meager existence alongside the flame. One night my clothes caught fire. I lived among the ashes for some time, shivering and whimpering. Let's say another four or five years. Sometimes I moaned, pretending to speak with the wind, but there was no one to answer me. Let's say I was the last one, that time. Let's say that and say no more about it.

Forty-nine minor angels have passed
through our memory, one per narract.
These are their names.